THE
HACKER'S
KEY

THE HACKER'S KEY

Jon Skovron

SCHOLASTIC INC.

This book is a work of fiction. Names, characters, places, and incidents are
either the product of the author's imagination or are used fictitiously, and any
resemblance to actual persons, living or dead, business establishments, events,
or locales is entirely coincidental.

ISBN 978-1-338-63398-6

10 9 8 7 6 5 4 3 2 1   20 21 22 23 24

Printed in the U.S.A.   40

First printing 2020

Book design by Baily Crawford

For my sons, Logan and Zane

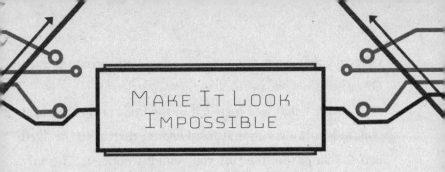

MAKE IT LOOK
IMPOSSIBLE

There was a small island off the southwestern coast of Iceland where the sky was gray, the sea was a slightly darker shade of gray, and the small strip of beach was made of black sand. The only way to get to this island was by boat or helicopter, which wasn't generally a problem because it was always cold and wet and not the sort of island you would want to visit anyway.

The island had only one building: a small wooden shack with one door and two windows. The paint on the shack had once been blue, but it was so faded from the salty sea air that it almost blended in with the gray sky. The salt-streaked windows looked like they hadn't been cleaned in years. The only thing that looked new was the lock on the door, which was so bright and shiny, it might have been installed yesterday. It was a magnetic lock that was impossible to pick.

The door was wide open.

Inside the shack were two small beds, a small table, a small refrigerator, and a small potbellied stove. Lying on the floor were two large men dressed as fishermen. They were not really fishermen, but instead United Nations elite guards. Or rather, they had been. Now they were dead.

A secret hatch was installed in the floor of the shack. It was hidden by a rug and insulated so that if you walked across that part of the rug, you wouldn't notice it. The only way you could have found it was if you already knew it was there. And even if you somehow learned of the hatch's existence, it was locked with a retinal scanner keyed to only three people on the planet.

The rug had been pulled up, and the hatch was open.

If you had somehow managed to locate the remote shack, pick the magnetic lock, eliminate the elite guards, discover the secret hatch, and bypass the retinal scanner, you would find a ladder that led down into an underground room. Once you reached the bottom, you had ten seconds to walk over to the sealed door at the far end of the room and speak into the microphone. If the vocal recognition software accepted you, the door opened. If it rejected you, the room was flooded with poison gas and you died quickly and painlessly. As with the retinal scanner, there were only three people on the planet that the vocal recognition software would accept.

The door was open.

On the other side of the door was a small chamber no bigger than a closet. In this small chamber was a table. On the table was a bulletproof case. On the case was a thumbprint scanner that was keyed to unlock the case only for those same three people.

The case was open, and the object that had been inside was gone. An old video game cartridge from the 1980s had been left in its place.

Most strikingly, all three people who had access to the case—one in Washington, one in Moscow, and one in Beijing—had been found dead in their homes the previous night, seemingly from heart attacks, several hours before the object had been stolen.

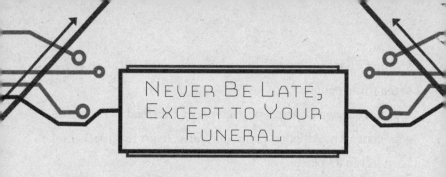

The moment Ada Genet awoke, she knew she had over-slept. There was way too much sunlight streaming into her small dorm room for six in the morning. She leaned over the side and looked at the lower bunk. Her Chilean roommate, Cody Francesco, was already gone. Ada and Cody didn't get along, so it was no surprise she hadn't tried to wake her before leaving. It was even possible Cody had sabotaged her alarm.

Ada flipped gracefully down from the top bunk and snatched up her watch from the table. Just as she'd thought, it was 6:55. She had five minutes to reach her classroom or Mr. Albertson would finally give her that demerit he'd been threatening. If she received one more demerit, she would lose what little freedom she had left.

Ada had been attending Springfield Military Reform School for almost a year now, but she still found it difficult to wake up early. When she'd lived with her father, they'd rarely risen before noon. She also found it difficult to go to bed before three in the morning for the same reason. She understood that one problem led to the other, but it just didn't seem right wasting so much beautiful nighttime with sleep. Her father would have agreed. But her father was in a supermax prison now, so he wasn't much help.

She wondered, a little resentfully, if he at least got to sleep late.

Ada dressed in her school uniform: white button-up shirt, blue-striped tie, tan skirt, blue knee-high socks, and blue blazer. She brushed her long blond hair and tied it back into a ponytail, then grabbed her backpack and peeked out into the hallway.

The hall monitor, Ms. Grand, stood in the middle of the passageway with her arms folded, looking around balefully beneath thick gray brows. Getting to class on time was already going to be a challenge, but if Ada tried to get past Ms. Grand, she'd no doubt receive a lecture that would guarantee she'd be late. She'd have to take the alternate route. And on such a cold morning, too . . .

Ada ducked back into her dorm room and took a small homemade device from her jacket pocket. It was slightly larger than a quarter and made from two discarded pieces of hard plastic that sandwiched a small circuit board. It was a simple radio frequency transmitter that her friend Jace had made for her. By squeezing the two pieces of plastic, it created a momentary connection on the circuit board that sent

5

a signal to Jace's RF receiver. She quickly squeezed out the following message in Morse code:

CQD SOS PLN W II SOS PLN W

Which meant: "All stations, distress call: This is an emergency. Enact Plan W. I repeat, this is an emergency. Enact Plan W."

Unfortunately, Ada could only send signals, not receive them, so she'd just have to hope Jace got the message. She took off her stiff leather school shoes and shoved them in her backpack. Then she opened the window, removed the screen, and climbed through.

Her dorm room was on the tenth floor. As she stepped onto the narrow stone ledge in blue-socked feet, she could see the school grounds stretched out below. This side of the building faced the large swath of green that served as the field for both football and American football. A chilly spring wind gusted past, ruffling her skirt and pulling at her ponytail.

"Four across, three down." She muttered the location of her homeroom to herself, trying to calm her nerves. She'd never actually climbed this building before.

Horizontal movement was simple enough. The dorm rooms on this floor were so narrow, all it took was a long stretch, a quick hop, and she was at the next window. In a few moments she had traversed all four. Now for the tricky bit: descending three floors slowly, rather than plummeting the full ten.

She pressed her stomach against the window and spread her stance as wide as she could. Then she squatted down and gripped the ledge beneath her feet with both hands. She lowered herself until her arms were straight and her feet dangled in front of the window on the next floor down. She stretched her feet out to either side and pressed them against opposite sides of the window frame. In climbing terminology, this was called stemming. She let go of the ledge above so that her hands were free and she was holding her entire weight with her outstretched legs. The muscles of her compact, acrobat's body strained as she balanced for a moment. So far, so good.

But she was accustomed to climbing in proper footwear, so she was not prepared when the thin fabric of her socks tore. Her feet slipped an inch.

Her stomach lurched into her throat, and her breath came in rapid gasps. Not good. She needed to calm down. Her legs were burning with fatigue from holding her weight in such an awkward way, but a climber should never act out of desperation. So she gritted her teeth, closed her eyes, and waited until she got her breath back under control. Only then did she grasp the window frame with her hands and shimmy down to the next ledge.

She let her legs recover for a few seconds. Then she repeated the process two more times. Though her socks were ruined and her limbs shook with exhaustion, she made it to the window outside her homeroom.

Now for the moment of truth. Had Jace gotten her signal and unlocked the window? Ada really hoped so, because she didn't have a backup plan. Her father would have been terribly disappointed in that.

She reached down, gripped the window sash, and pulled. It slid smoothly open. She allowed herself a quick sigh of relief. Then she slipped into the classroom just as the bell rang.

Mr. Albertson sat at his desk at the front of the room, his broad forehead wrinkled in concentration as he graded papers. Cody Francesco's perfectly bronzed face looked smug as she watched him. When the bell went off, Cody turned back to look at what she no doubt expected to be Ada's empty seat. The whole thing was almost worth it to see Cody's smirk melt into openmouthed shock when she saw Ada slide into her desk beside Jace and pull her shoes on over her tattered socks.

Ada smiled cheerfully at Cody, then turned to Jace.

"I owe you one."

Jace Winslow had brown skin and the fuzzy beginnings of a mustache. His dense black hair was shaved into a tight fade on the sides but splayed out on top in short, thick twists. He grinned at her. "Samus, you really are nuts."

He'd given her that nickname the day they met because he said she looked like Samus Aran, the galactic bounty hunter from the *Metroid* and *Super Smash Bros.* video game series. Ada had known right then that they'd get along fine.

"How am I crazy?" she asked as she straightened her tie.

"Plan *Window*? I did *not* think you would ever actually do it."

"I'm down to my last demerit. There's no way I'm getting transferred to C Class. They have chaperones at all times, and I need my alone time. I'm just glad you got my message."

"Without phones, it's all I've got. Speaking of, I'm almost done with that two-way I've been working on. It should be ready—"

"All right, class." Mr. Albertson looked up from his papers. "The bell has rung, so let's settle down and . . ." He frowned thoughtfully at Ada. "Miss Genet, when did you arrive?"

She gave him an innocent look. "I've been here all along, Mr. Albertson."

"Hmmm . . ." His eyes moved to the window and his frown deepened. "And why is the window open?"

She'd forgotten to close the window! Only a year at this school, and she was already starting to lose her edge. "Oh, I opened it just now, Mr. Albertson. I love that fresh morning air, don't you?"

"Hmmm . . ." he said again, not looking convinced. Probably because Ada was known to loudly complain about mornings on a daily basis. But as suspicious as it was, he didn't have enough proof to accuse her of anything, and he knew it. So he just sighed. "Fine. Whatever. Let's begin—"

"Sorry to interrupt you, Mr. Albertson."

A woman in her early forties with short black hair and silver-framed glasses stuck her head in through the door. Ada's chest tightened. It was her caseworker. And Ms. North never interrupted a class with good news. Did she have any other students in here? Ada really hoped so . . .

Mr. Albertson gave the caseworker an unfriendly look. "Yes, Ms. North, what is it?"

In general, the teachers and caseworkers at Springfield Military Reform School didn't get along, probably because teachers were there to help students, at least theoretically, while caseworkers were there to make things harder. Supposedly, somewhere between the teaching and the punishing, students were reformed and made upstanding members of society. But Ada didn't buy it.

Ms. North's cold blue eyes shifted from Mr. Albertson to Ada, and she smiled. The only time Ada ever saw Ms. North smile was when she was in trouble.

"I'm afraid I must speak with Ms. Genet," Ms. North said in her calm, crisp voice. "In private. Immediately."

A s Ada followed Ms. North down the hall to the guidance offices, she wondered how she'd been caught scaling the side of the building. There hadn't been time for any of her classmates to tell on her. Maybe someone had glanced out a window and saw her? Or maybe she'd been picked up by a security camera outside the building?

But Ms. North hadn't said anything about it yet, so for now Ada would play dumb. Like her father always said, never give anything away, even if you think they have you.

Springfield Military Reform School was basically a minimum-security prison for teens disguised as a school. But the "guidance offices" didn't even bother with the disguise. As soon as Ada and Ms. North passed through the main door into the guidance wing, the cheerful motivational and safety posters vanished, leaving only blank white walls and a room that looked more like an office than a school.

Men and women in business attire sat working at desks in rows. Those were the lower-ranking caseworkers, called junior counselors, who each handled anywhere from ten to twenty of the "low-risk" B Class students. Students like Cody

Francesco and Jace Winslow. The higher-ranking case-workers, called senior counselors, had a smaller case load but handled "high-risk" students, nearly all of whom were in C Class. Ada was one of the few students in B Class who had a senior counselor. It was like they were expecting her to screw up and get sent to C Class any day. Maybe this would be that day.

Ada followed Ms. North to her office in the back of the room. All senior counselors had their own private offices, and it was a sure bet that if one of them brought a student into their office and shut the door, it was bad news.

Ada sat down in the chair facing the desk and watched as Ms. North closed the door.

Ms. North walked unhurriedly over and sat down. She steepled her hands, and when she looked at Ada, the overhead light glared off her glasses in a way that made it difficult to see her eyes.

Ada knew this was all done to intimidate her. And even though it was sort of working, she refused to show it, keeping her expression cool and disinterested.

"Ms. Genet, do you know how long I have worked at Springfield Military Reform School?"

Any guess, too low or too high, might be considered offensive. So Ada simply said, "No, ma'am."

"Ten years as a junior counselor, and eight as a senior

counselor, for a total of eighteen years. And during these past eighteen years, one policy has always held firm. If a convicted felon has groomed their child to continue the . . . *family trade*, if you will, the guidance staff at Springfield Military Reform School strongly recommends that the child have no contact with the convicted parent until such time as the child's counselor deems them reformed and no longer susceptible to the influences of said parent."

"That's why you won't let me visit my father in prison," said Ada. "Even though he's only an hour's drive away."

Ms. North nodded. "I'm glad you recall. Because you will then appreciate what a special circumstance this is when I tell you that in ten minutes, a transport will arrive to take you to see your father."

"R-really?"

"Really." Ms. North never looked particularly happy, but she looked even less happy about this. Was she bitter because she'd been telling Ada for the past year that she'd never see her father again, and now she'd been proven wrong? Or was there something else going on here? Ada had expected punishment for climbing the building, not an offer to finally see her father. It seemed far too good to be true. There had to be a catch.

"Why now?" she asked.

Ms. North nodded, as if she'd expected that question.

"Astute as ever, Ms. Genet. Your exemption from the policy is not out of some sentimental weakness on the part of the United States government. We have need of you."

"You want *me* to help *you*?" If Ada hadn't been afraid of blowing her chances of seeing her father, she would have laughed in the woman's face.

"Yesterday, something . . . *dangerous* was stolen from a top secret United Nations facility. So far, our only clue to its current whereabouts points directly to your father."

"But my father has been in a supermax prison for the last year."

"Correct," said Ms. North. "We do not believe he perpetrated the crime, but we do suspect he knows the person who did. He might even have some idea what they plan to do with the . . . stolen object."

Ada did not like where this was going. She said nothing.

"We've already interrogated him, of course," continued Ms. North. "However, he refuses to speak to anyone but you."

Ada tried to keep the anger out of her voice but failed. "You want me to *interrogate my own father*?"

"We've told him that if he cooperates in this investigation, you will be granted monthly visitation rights, so he has plenty of incentive." She pushed her glasses up on her nose and scowled. "To be clear, that was offered to him despite my objections. Frankly, I think the last thing you need is communication with your father. But I have been overruled by my superiors, which tells you just how important this is."

Monthly visitation with her father was tempting, but Ada didn't like the idea of trying to get things out of him for the government. It felt like betrayal.

"What if I said I didn't want to do it?" she asked.

Ms. North smiled coldly. "Well then, I suppose I'd have to tell Mr. Albertson about your adventure scaling the side of the building this morning to avoid another tardy. I believe that would force him to give you the final demerit you've been dreading."

Ada glared at Ms. North. She *had* known about Ada sneaking into class that morning and had just been saving it to use as leverage.

Ms. North didn't seem bothered by Ada's hostility. "So do we have a deal?"

It was clear the government needed Ada's father, if they cut a deal with him for visitation rights. Now they needed *her*, as well. Her father always said if someone needs you, make certain you get something in return.

"You know," Ada said casually, "studies suggest that positive reinforcement is a much better motivator for teens than the threat of punishment."

Ms. North's eyes narrowed. "What do you have in mind?"

"If I find out something useful, you will not only forget my climb this morning, you will also get rid of one of the demerits that are already on my record."

"Ms. Genet." Ms. North leaned forward. "If you get actionable intel—something we can really use—I will wipe your whole slate clean. I will even consider allowing that video game club you and Jace have been petitioning for since the beginning of the school year. How's that for motivation?"

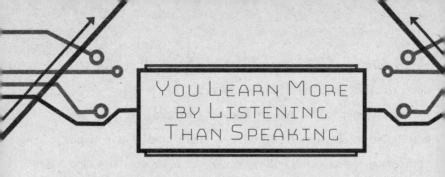
Ten minutes later, Ada and Ms. North were sitting in the back of a black SUV with tinted windows. A metal screen separated them from the driver in the front seat. There were no barred windows or cage doors on the Springfield campus, so when Ada saw the screen, it was a jarring reminder of how little freedom she truly had.

Ms. North caught her eyeing the door.

"If you're wondering, they don't open from the inside."

"I wasn't." Ada might want to escape, but she wanted to see her father more.

She stared out the window at the farms and scraggly clusters of trees that passed for landscape in this part of Virginia. To the northeast, she knew, was Washington, DC. Beyond that was Baltimore, Maryland, where Jace grew up. The closest city to the south was Richmond, Virginia, followed by Raleigh, North Carolina. To the west was the beginning of the Appalachian Mountains, and to the east was Chesapeake Bay and then the Atlantic Ocean. Visualizing a map in her mind had always made her feel better. Probably because she and her father had traveled so much, it had been easy at times to feel adrift, almost like she was disconnected from the real world. Maps had grounded her. They had reminded her that she was real, and not some kind of ghost . . .

"We're here. Ms. Genet?"

Ada snapped out of her reverie and saw that they were approaching a massive concrete building surrounded by an equally massive stone wall. Razor wire stretched across the top of the wall, with guard towers interspersed at regular intervals. There were prison guards armed with automatic rifles stationed at each tower. While it was certainly intimidating, she was surprised by how . . . *dull* it looked. Not at all like the prisons in movies that housed criminal masterminds. And her father was unquestionably one of those.

Their black SUV pulled up to the guard station before the wall's thick metal gate. The driver, a dark-skinned man with a shiny bald head, rolled down his window and showed his ID. The guard nodded and pushed a button, and then the metal gate slowly swung open. Ada looked over the gate carefully for vulnerabilities, more out of habit than anything else.

The courtyard between the wall and the building was empty except for a small cluster of parked black SUVs that looked just like theirs. The driver pulled their SUV to join the rest and cut the engine.

Ada and Ms. North had to wait until the driver came around and opened the door. Then the three of them walked over to an unmarked door on the side of the building. The driver touched his ID card on a pad next to the door. It lit up green and the door unlocked with an audible click. Ada was surprised that a supermax facility would be using such feeble technology. She could have spoofed a card for a proximity reader like that with a smartphone and ten dollars' worth of hardware.

The driver pushed the door open. Ada followed Ms. North down an empty hallway lit with the sort of old-fashioned fluorescents that made everyone look like they had been dead for about an hour. How old *was* this facility? Could such a place really even hold her father?

The driver didn't follow them, remaining instead by the door. As he stood there with his hands clasped in front of him, Ada noticed the distinct bulge in his suit jacket that indicated he had a gun. She also noticed that he was missing the little finger on his left hand. Something about that detail tickled her memory, but she couldn't quite recall what it was.

Ms. North stopped at a door about halfway down the hall and knocked.

There was a brief pause, and then a deep male voice said, "Come in."

Ms. North opened the door and Ada followed her into a small, crowded room. Four men and one woman, all dressed in suits, huddled around a single laptop on a small table.

"Ah, Special Agent North," said an older American man with a salt-and-pepper crew cut.

Ada looked at Ms. North. *Agent?*

Ms. North glanced at her, raising a thin black eyebrow in response. It seemed to say, "Oops." Then she turned back at the man.

"Sir, here is Genet's daughter, Ada, as requested. If I may reiterate—"

"Yes, yes, against your better judgement. I recall." The man waved his hand dismissively and turned back to the computer screen.

Ada assumed this must be Ms. North's boss. While she had never liked Ms. North, she liked how rude her boss was even less. But a slight movement on the laptop screen caught Ada's eye and all other thoughts fled.

She was looking at a live feed of her father in his cell.

"Papa . . ." The word leapt from her mouth before she could stop it, and her stomach twisted as she stared at the person who she loved most in the world trapped in a tiny room.

His long, lean frame was stretched out on a bunk as he read a battered paperback of one of his favorite novels, *Neuromancer* by William Gibson. It was strange to see him wearing an orange prison jumpsuit, since she had never known him to wear bright colors. Black, gray, navy blue, hunter green, perhaps brown now and then. Those were the colors of Monsieur Remy Genet, internationally renowned hacker and thief. He'd lost weight, too. Perhaps it was the harsh lighting in his small, unadorned cell, but he looked almost gaunt, with hollows in his cheeks and dark circles beneath his eyes. Thankfully, the eyes themselves were the same. Bright green eyes that sparkled with amusement and more than a little mischief . . .

All at once, Ada's throat tightened up and she had to blink back tears.

"Tch, this whole plan is absurd," a tall, broad-shouldered man said in Russian to the short bald man beside him. "What do we hope to get from this *child* besides hysterics?"

Ada wheeled on him, her face flushed with anger. In perfect Russian, she said, "This *young woman* will get you actionable intel, so you can just go to the bathhouse!"

Telling someone to go to the bathhouse in Russian was a lot ruder than it sounded, and judging by the man's shocked expression, he was well aware of that. However, the bald man next to him chuckled.

In heavily accented English, the bald Russian said to Ms. North's boss, "General Pendleton, it looks like you have made the right choice after all. She seems well equipped to handle herself."

Pendleton nodded tersely. "Genet groomed this girl as his successor practically since infancy, Mr. Shukhov."

The remaining man and woman in the room were Chinese. The man was perhaps thirty years old and quite thin, with slicked-back hair. The woman was a little older than Ms. North, with streaks of gray in her shoulder-length black hair. The two had remained silent before, but now the woman spoke in precise, British-inflected English.

"Our government believes the daughter to have been an accomplice in Genet's criminal activity as early as age five. By age twelve, she was successfully running point on some of his smaller operations. While that is . . . *impressive*, how can we be certain she is trustworthy?"

Pendleton shrugged. "Does it matter, Ms. Wang? As long as she gets him to talk, she's served her purpose. Then we send her back to the reform program that we *all* agreed was best for her."

"Hmm." Ms. Wang's expression suggested that while she had agreed to it, she most definitely did not think it was best. Her countryman leaned over and whispered something in her ear, and she nodded but said nothing more.

Ada did *not* like being talked about as if she wasn't in the room, and she didn't try to hide her scowl when Pendleton turned back to her. But he either didn't notice or didn't care.

"Have you ever heard of the Hacker's Key, Miss Genet?"

She shook her head.

"It's a dangerous . . . let's call it a crypto tool. Until

recently, it had been kept by the United Nations at a secret location off the coast of Iceland. It was protected by top-of-the-line security systems."

"Better than this museum, you mean," said Ada.

Shukhov snorted and covered his mouth as if stifling a laugh. Pendleton did not look so amused.

"We *all* thought that infiltration into the location was impossible." He looked around at the other adults for a moment, as if daring one of them to disagree. None did, and even Shukhov looked a little embarrassed. Pendleton turned back to Ada. "And yet somehow the Key was stolen yesterday by a person or persons unknown. The only clue was an old video game cartridge left at the scene. Hand written on the cartridge in permanent marker were the words 'For Remy.'"

"What game?" asked Ada.

Pendleton gave her a confused look, like he didn't think the game itself mattered. "It was . . ."

"*Metroid*, published in 1986 by Nintendo," said Ms. Wang.

"Yes, that was it," said Pendleton. Then his eyes narrowed. "Why, does that mean something to you?"

Ada shrugged. "It's my father's favorite game. Whoever left it for him knows him quite well."

"I see . . ." Pendleton and Ms. North exchanged a strange look. "Anyway, the nature of the Key, and the apparent impossibility of the theft—so similar to his own style—led us to believe that the 'Remy' referenced on the game cartridge is your father and that he is somehow involved."

"Or it could be misdirection," said Ada. "After all, why would the thief give you anything that would help you catch them?"

He nodded. "That's what we thought at first, but it seemed safest to question your father anyway, since we already have him in custody. Generally, your father loves to talk. We can't shut him up, in fact. But when we asked him about the Hacker's Key and showed him the game, he suddenly went quiet. That's when we started thinking maybe we have something after all."

"So you don't really know anything," said Ada. "You just want me to go fishing."

Pendleton didn't look happy about that summary, but he nodded. "Essentially, yes."

"What does this Key do, exactly?"

"That information," said Ms. Wang, "is on a need-to-know basis."

"Yes, it shouldn't be directly relevant to your task, Miss Genet," said Pendleton. "So how about it? Are you ready to start making amends for your past misdeeds?"

Ada turned to Ms. North. "Our agreement still stands?"

She nodded.

"Agreement?" asked Pendleton.

"It shouldn't be directly relevant to your task, General Pendleton," Ada told him, and was rewarded by another snicker from Shukhov.

"I'm sorry I can't tell you any details about the Key," said Pendleton, not looking particularly sorry. "But I can tell you that a lot of lives are at stake here. Don't let him run the conversation. Get us something we can use."

"No one can get something from my father that he doesn't wish to give, but I'll try."

Ms. North held open the door to the hallway. "This way, Ms. Genet."

As Ada walked toward the door, Shukhov touched her lightly on the shoulder. He said in Russian, "It's a shame you lost your temper and spoke up so quickly. Who knows what you might have learned if you hadn't been so eager to show off."

Ada stared at him a moment, feeling her cheeks flush with shame. Of course he was right. If she'd pretended not to understand what people were saying, she might have learned a lot of useful information. Her father would have been disappointed in her shortsightedness.

Feeling humbled, she followed Ms. North out into the hallway and to an elevator. Once the elevator doors had closed and they began to ascend, Ada turned to Ms. North and asked something that she'd been wondering since their arrival.

"Are all Springfield counselors government agents?"

Ms. North sighed. "I wish Pendleton had been a little more discreet about that."

"Well?" pressed Ada. "Are they?"

"Only the senior counselors."

"The junior counselors are training to become agents?"

"Some of them," admitted Ms. North.

"What *is* Springfield Military Reform School?" asked Ada.

"What indeed," said Ms. North, her tone making it clear she was done answering questions.

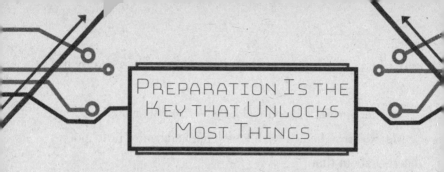

The room was divided in half by a clear, plexiglass wall. On the near side were a couple of plastic chairs for visitors, and on the far side of the glass was Ada's father's cell. It was just large enough for a bed and a toilet.

Her father had discarded his book and now sat on the edge of his bunk, his eyes fixed on Ada as she walked into the room, followed by Ms. North.

"Ah, ma petite chou," he said in a faint French accent that he could discard at any time but generally chose not to. "How beautiful you have grown in only a year."

She sat down in one of the chairs and looked at him. "Papa, you should eat more."

He shrugged. "The food they serve here . . . I would not call it truly eating." Then he looked at Ms. North and smiled in that cold way he did to people he didn't like. "Excuse me, madam, but I believe my one condition on speaking was that it be to my daughter *alone*, s'il vous plaît."

Ms. North's expression hardened. "For the well-being of this girl, I cannot in good conscience—"

A speaker in the upper left corner of the room crackled to life.

"Allow it, Agent North," came Pendleton's deep voice. "That's an order."

Ms. North glared at Ada's father. "You know they're all watching you anyway."

Ada's father nodded. "It at least grants us the illusion of privacy, which is better than nothing."

It was an odd thing for her father to say. He generally was not interested in illusion and was dismissive of people who were. It was so out of character that it made Ada wonder if he was up to something. But what could it be?

Ms. North turned to Ada, still looking irritated. "I will be just outside the door. If you need a break, or want to leave, just knock and I'll open it immediately."

Then she turned sharply on her heel and left the room, yanking the door closed behind her.

"They will have locked it from the outside, naturally," her father said nonchalantly.

"I expect so, Papa."

It felt strange sitting there with her father. It had been so long, and she'd wanted to see him so badly. To tell him how hard it was at the school. How most of her teachers were dull and most of her classmates were stupid. How much she hated all of it and wished the two of them could go back to the way things used to be, when they'd been free to roam the world, having adventures and outsmarting the law at every turn. But now, as she looked into his green eyes, she understood that she didn't need to say anything. He knew and felt the same way.

His voice was sad, but he held on to his smile as he said, "I may never be able to leave this place, chérie."

"Don't say that, Papa. Maybe if you cooperate with these people and tell them how to get this Key thing back, they'll shorten your sentence."

He leaned back in his cot and closed his eyes. "Maybe they would . . ." Then his eyes opened and he gave her that twinkling, mischievous look she knew so well. "But I have a better idea."

"Yeah?" she said eagerly.

"*Yeah?*" he drawled in an exaggerated American accent. "You have been in this country too long, chérie."

"I've adapted, just as you taught me," she said frostily.

"Of course, of course." He put his hands behind his head, seeming more relaxed with each moment. "Have you made any friends?"

"I have." Just Jace, really, but he was worth at least five regular people. Did enemies count? If so, then perhaps Cody, as well.

Her father nodded. "Bien. And you are learning things

at this school? Getting along well with your teachers?"

"Well enough."

He smiled briefly at that, as if he knew, or at least guessed, how close to *not* getting along she was.

Normally he was not the sort of person who asked such boring, impersonal questions. What was he up to?

Then his expression grew serious. "Chérie, do you know why *Metroid* is so important to me?"

She gave him a searching look. Was he starting to hint at the Hacker's Key? She couldn't tell.

"Because it introduced the concept of open exploration and discovery in platform video games?" she asked.

He gave her a faint smile. "That was important to the history of video games, ma petite chou, but it is not why *I* think it's important. You must remember, when I was a child in the eighties, female characters in video games were merely princesses to be rescued. Never anything more. And I thought nothing of that, because I did not know better. Even when I began playing *Metroid*, I did not know Samus Aran was a woman. She wore a helmet, after all, and since there was nothing to suggest otherwise, I assumed Samus was a man. It wasn't until after weeks of playing, when I finally beat the evil Mother Brain, that Samus's helmet came off, and I was shocked to discover that all this time, while I had been saving the galaxy, I had been a *girl*." He laughed quietly. "Ma chérie,

I cannot tell you what a revelation that was. How . . . *important* it felt to me then."

He gazed at her for a moment. His expression was unreadable, but his eyes glistened with intensity.

"And how important it feels to me right now."

He was trying to tell her something. She was sure of it. If only she understood what it was.

"Papa, are we going to talk about this Hacker's Key?"

"The Root Key?" His expression suddenly became bored. "It is an old story. And so very tedious. Tell me, do you remember those American talk shows where, in the middle of the program, the host suddenly announces that certain lucky people in the audience have something special beneath their chair?" He closed his eyes and smiled again. "They are always so surprised. I wonder why no one ever thinks to check beneath their chair . . ."

She knew, without a doubt, that there was something beneath her chair. She thought back to the video feed that the agents were watching. She hadn't seen any plastic chairs in the frame, so they probably couldn't actually see her right now, only hear her.

"Yes, Papa, we used to love watching those shows together."

That was not true at all, but she needed the agents to think they were just having a casual conversation while she leaned sideways and reached under her chair. She felt a small canvas pouch taped to the underside, and her heart quickened in a way not even climbing the side of the school building had managed. A new adventure? But what was it?

"Do you remember the episode where people found car keys?" her father asked. "That was my favorite. Although sadly you would be too young to appreciate such a thing."

As her father rambled on about talk shows, cars, and the risks of allowing teenagers to drive, all to distract Pendleton and his cronies, Ada slowly peeled the canvas pouch from the bottom of the chair, careful not to let the tape make any noise as it came free. Inside she found a folding multi-tool and a small, homemade electronic device she recognized at once as a Wi-Fi scrambler.

Ada stared down at the scrambler, a small black plastic rectangle with a single button. Wi-Fi operated at a frequency of either 2.4 or 5 GHz. While 5 GHz was faster, it had a shorter range and didn't pass through thick walls. The laptop that the agents were watching from downstairs had not been plugged in to anything, which meant they were receiving the feed wirelessly. To get through these thick prison walls, the wireless signal would need to be broadcasting at the 2.4 GHz frequency.

The problem with using 2.4 GHz was that a lot of other things emitted a signal on that frequency. Baby monitors, cordless landline phones, even microwave ovens. Back when all consumer Wi-Fi had been 2.4 GHz, if a poorly insulated microwave happened to broadcast on the same channel as a person's wireless access point, that person would be surprised to find that their internet connection went down every time they reheated leftovers.

A Wi-Fi scrambler made use of this vulnerability by using a multi-channel architecture to blast interference across all eleven channels on the 2.4 GHz frequency, distorting nearby Wi-Fi signals on that frequency for a short period of time. Signals like the one the agents downstairs were using to observe her father's cell.

Ada held the scrambler in her palm, her thumb hovering over the button. She looked at her father and saw that his eyes were bright and eager.

"Papa, will you be ready for me to drive when it's time?" Of course, that wasn't really the question she was asking.

He shrugged calmly. "I am ready whenever you are, ma petite chou."

She pressed the button.

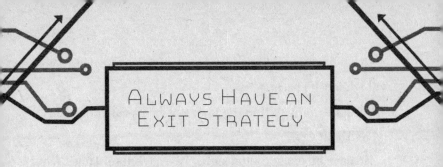

"Okay, chérie, there isn't much time, so listen to me closely."

Ada's father was on his feet, his casual, relaxed pose gone. "Open the ventilation cover while I tell you what you will do next."

Ada went into action without hesitation. It was just like old times. She stacked the chairs on top of each other so that she could reach the ventilation shaft near the ceiling on the side wall. She unfolded the multi-tool, selected the screwdriver head, and began to work on the screws that held the cover in place.

"How will we get you out of there, Papa?"

Her father laughed. "Oh, you misunderstand, chérie. I'm not the one escaping. *You* are."

She stopped working on the vent and looked down at him. "What?"

He made a flipping motion with his hand. "Keep going. We only have a few minutes before they get the signal back or come running up here to check on us. In either case, you must be gone by then."

35

"But why, Papa?" She turned back to the vent cover. "What will I do once I escape?"

"You are going to find the Root Key before anyone else."

"Without *you*?"

He gave an exasperated sigh. "Yes, of course! That's what I was telling you, my little Samus. You don't need me. You're ready for your first real mission."

"But—"

"Shush. Keep working and I will tell you all that I wish to tell you. Follow the ventilation system down to the first floor, where Pascale is waiting for you downstairs with the car."

"Pascale?" Of course. Now Ada remembered what had been bothering her about the driver missing a finger on his left hand. Her father's old friend Pascale was missing that same finger. Then she frowned. "But, Papa, he didn't look like—"

"Yes, yes. We sprung for some facial prosthetics. He even shaved his head. Only the best for my daughter's breakout. Now listen, Pascale will give you a passport and some money, then drop you off in Baltimore. Make your way to Cairnes Lane behind the bookshop in Hampden, where you'll find one of our safe houses. I trust you remember the passcode system?"

"Of course, Papa." She took the cover off the vent and placed it on the floor, careful not to make any loud noise that might alert Ms. North in the hallway.

"*Très bien*. You will find everything else you need in the safe house to begin tracking the thief."

"What should I do with the Key when I—"

"No time for that, ma petite chou. You're a big girl now. Figure it out for yourself."

"But—"

"And most importantly . . ." His eyes narrowed. "Mademoiselle Genet, never underestimate *family*."

She had no idea what he meant, but felt it was important. "Y-yes, Papa."

"Now go! Va vite!"

She placed one foot on the top of the chair back and prepared to jump up into the shaft. But then she paused. She was leaving her father already, and she didn't know when she'd be able to see him again.

"It doesn't feel right, leaving you here like this."

He looked amused. "I should hope not. But if you don't go now, all my hard work will be for nothing."

"Je t'aime, Papa."

"And I love you, ma petite chouchou."

Then she leapt up into the vent and began crawling along the passage, leaving her father behind to deal with the very irate agents who would soon be coming through the door.

Samus Aran, the galactic bounty hunter in the *Metroid* games, had a cool exoskeletal suit that let her turn into a morph ball so she could easily roll through tight spaces and down narrow tunnels. As Ada squirmed along the ventilation shaft, she wished, not for the first time in her life, that she could turn into a morph ball, too.

Ada had always hated crawling through ventilation shafts. The darkness, the hot, stuffy air, the metallic sound of her breath, the inability to turn or move in any direction but forward. And of course, there was the ever-present chance of spiders. A tickle of panic accompanied her hurried movements, and she had to force herself to take slow, deep breaths of the dusty air so she didn't hyperventilate. To distract herself, she wondered why her father wanted her to find the Key. To prove herself? Some sort of rite of passage? But what was she supposed to do with the Key if she got it? She didn't even know what the stupid thing did. So maybe that was the first thing to figure out.

Well, once she had actually escaped from prison.

Even though Ada hated wriggling through ventilation

systems, she had done it many times, and fortunately, they all seemed to share the same basic design. Despite crawling blindly through the dark, she was able to find her way down to the ground floor pretty quickly. From there she worked her way through the vents over to an opening that was close to the side door where Pascale still waited. She hoped.

She squirmed around in the tight shaft so that she could pull the multi-tool out of her jacket pocket, but before she could begin working the vent cover loose, she heard a door open below her, followed by several sets of rapid footsteps.

"Perhaps it is simply a technical issue," she heard Shukhov say.

"I'm telling you, that wily Frenchman is up to something . . ." Pendleton's voice replied as it trailed away with the footsteps.

It would only take a few more minutes for them to get to the top floor and discover that she'd escaped. Speed was now more important than stealth. Once she was certain they'd all gotten into the elevator, she used both feet to kick out the cover. It clanged loudly as it hit the ground and she dropped down into the hallway.

Ada turned expectantly toward the exit, but Pascale was no longer stationed at the door. Instead it was some white guy, and he did not look friendly.

"You there! Don't move!"

Ada's father was a concerned and loving parent, but until recently he had also led a very dangerous life. And so, primarily for his own peace of mind, he had insisted that she begin training with some of the world's best hand-to-hand combat experts at the age of five.

"Get down on your knees with your hands behind your head!" shouted the guard as he reached for the gun holstered beneath his jacket.

"No thanks," Ada said, then sprinted toward him.

The guard clearly hadn't been expecting a young girl to rush him, and he fumbled with his gun for a moment. That was all she needed.

Ada leapt into a front aerial flip. As her feet came down, she knocked his gun out of his hand with her left heel. Still in the air, she twisted her torso and swung her right knee into the side of his head, sending him reeling. She landed behind him on all fours, then swept his legs out from under him. His head hit the floor loud enough to make her wince. She hoped he wasn't hurt too badly, but she didn't have time to check.

She snatched up the ID card that hung from his belt and swiped it across the proximity reader. As soon as the door unlocked, she dropped the ID and ran out into the courtyard.

The group of black SUVs were still there, and she saw the driver from before crouching down beside one, letting the air out of its tires.

"Pascale?" she asked dubiously.

He glanced over at her, and then burst into a grin.

"Ha! You didn't even recognize me!" he said in his liquid Haitian accent. He tore off the fake nose and chin, leaving a thin line of spirit gum where they'd been glued into place. But now he looked like the Pascale she remembered.

"It *is* you!"

"Of course! Come on, chérie. Let's go."

They hurried over to the SUV, and Ada took the front passenger seat this time. But as Pascale started the engine, a siren began to howl.

"Time's up," he muttered, and gunned the engine.

The iron gate was still closed. It was one problem after another, but instead of being discouraged, Ada felt her pulse pounding. At last, after months of enforced boredom, a proper adventure had begun.

"Hold on tight," said Pascale as he circled around to give himself some room to accelerate.

But Ada had scoped out the gate on her way in, so she knew that the bolts on the hinges were an inch thick. Assuming the standard tensile strength of an industrial bolt and taking into account Newton's second law of motion that force equals mass times acceleration, the roughly two-thousand-kilogram SUV would need to accelerate at around seven meters per second squared to generate enough force to break the hinges of the gate and knock it down. That was the same acceleration as a Ferrari sports car. She was pretty sure their SUV did not have that kind of pickup.

"Wait, Pascale! We won't—"

"Don't you trust me, Ada?"

She stared helplessly as Pascale laughed like a madman and slammed his foot on the gas, steering the SUV directly toward the gate. She braced herself, gripping the handlebar above the window so hard, her knuckles turned white. But she forced herself not to close her eyes. Never look away from danger. That's what her father always said.

The gate blew off its hinges like it was made of cheap plastic. Ada turned to the grinning Pascale. "How.. . ."

"While you were in there talking to your papa, I applied some nitric acid to the hinges. Just enough to weaken the metal without destroying it completely. Then, of course, as you saw, I let all the air out of the other vehicles' tires, so we shouldn't get any immediate pursuit."

Ada let out a sigh, her pulse returning to normal. "I'm sorry, Pascale. I shouldn't have doubted you."

He shrugged. "You've been out of the game a minute. I'll let it slide this time."

They sped along the empty highway for about a half hour, and Ada watched the small farms and empty fields fly past. Not many places to conceal a big SUV with government plates when the law finally caught up with them. What would they do then?

But again, she should have trusted Pascale. Because a few minutes later, they turned down a tree-lined dirt road that led to an old farmhouse with a detached barn. Pascale pulled into the barn, where a dingy gray two-door car with Virginia plates waited for them. A man in a plaid shirt with short red hair stood beside it. Pascale handed the man a wad of cash, and then he and Ada climbed into the small car.

The man waved cheerfully to them as they drove back along the dirt road to the highway. Ada rolled down the window and waved back, because it was the polite thing to do. Her father had always taught her that being an outlaw didn't mean being rude.

"Whoooo," sighed Pascale. "That should give us some space." Then he grinned at Ada again. "Welcome back to the world, chérie. We missed you."

Ada leaned back in her seat and stared at the open road before them. "It feels good to be free."

"On to Baltimore, then," he said.

"Not yet," she said. "I need to go back to school first."

His eyes widened. "It'd better be something important."

"Not something, some*one*," she said. "If I'm going to track down this Hacker's Key, the first thing I need to do is talk to a hacker."

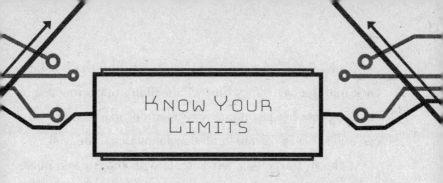

The RF transmitter Jace had given Ada, which broadcast at only 300 kHz, had a range of roughly one kilometer, or a little more than half a mile. Luckily, there was an office complex with a large parking lot directly across the highway from the school. As soon as they parked, Ada sent a message in Morse code, and then another every hour, asking Jace to meet her on the roof of the school at midnight. Technically the roof was off limits, but the door wasn't even locked, and the two of them had snuck up there many times during the past year when they needed a break from the oppressive atmosphere that seemed to permeate every room in the school.

While Ada waited for midnight to come, she looked through the small duffel bag that Pascale had pulled from the trunk of the car. It had a change of clothes, all dark colors, which would come in handy when she snuck onto school grounds that night. There was also an envelope of cash and a fake passport under the name "Amy Shaftoe," which was a character from another of her father's favorite novels, *Cryptonomicon* by Neal Stephenson.

"Drôle, Papa," she muttered as she stuffed the passport back into the bag. "Very funny." She didn't relish the idea of claiming that her last name was "Shaftoe" to a customs officer, and she was certain her father knew that quite well.

At eleven thirty, Ada left Pascale with the car and made her way to the school. Since it wasn't officially a prison, only run like one, there were no bars or razor-wire fences. The primary danger was being spotted by the security staff who regularly patrolled the grounds.

But this late at night, there was only a sliver of moonlight for security to see by, and she was now dressed in black jeans, black sneakers, fingerless black climbing gloves, and a dark gray hoodie. When she pulled the hood up to cover her golden hair, she was nearly invisible in the darkness. Even so, she kept to cover as often as possible, sneaking behind parked cars, a mailbox, and then the carefully manicured shrubs that lined the perimeter of the building.

She still wasn't sure how Ms. North had known about that morning's wall-crawling adventure. She scanned the outside of the building, looking for video cameras. She didn't see any, so perhaps she'd just been spotted by someone as she crossed a window. Well, lights-out for the school was ten o'clock, so she didn't think there was much danger of that now.

She waited until a security guard turned the corner, then

emerged from the bushes and quickly began climbing the side of the building.

Going straight up was much easier than sideways and down, especially now that she was wearing climbing gloves and flexible, thin-soled sneakers. She stepped onto the ledge of the first-floor window, reached up, and gripped the top. Just like she had done when climbing down, she pressed out to the sides with both feet so that she could reach the ledge on the window above. This time, her sneakers had enough grip to keep her securely anchored. Once she had a good grip on the next window ledge up, she lifted her legs and hooked her toes on the top of the lower window, rising slowly. She balanced on her toes, and this time stemmed with her hands. Her upper body wasn't as strong as her lower body, so she couldn't hold it long. But she only needed to pull her feet up the short distance to the next ledge. One story down, nine more to go.

Ten minutes later, she rolled onto the roof and heard a startled yelp.

"Samus? Is that you?"

"Hey, Jace."

Jace leaned against the brick wall by the door, his arms folded. He might have looked cool except his eyes were bugging out of his head. "Once again I must ask: Why are you so crazy?"

She pushed back her hood and smiled as she hurried over to him. "Listen, I don't have much time—"

"Wait, are you escaping? How come I didn't see you all day?"

"I already escaped," she told him. "But I need your help with something, so I came back. Then I'm leaving again, probably for good."

"I don't climb walls if that's what you want," he said quickly. "Up *or* down."

"No, Jace, I need information," she said. "Have you ever heard of the Hacker's Key?"

He laughed. "Oh sure."

"Why is that funny?"

"Well, I mean, it's a *hoax*," he said. "The Root Key, or the Hacker's Key, or whatever, is one of those dumb internet stories people spread online to freak each other out, you know?"

"Okay, but what is it?"

"*Supposedly*, way back in the day, at like the dawn of the computer age in the 1960s or whatever, they were already worried about artificial intelligence taking over one day. So the dudes at IBM wrote a tiny string of code into their source that could act as a fail-safe. If an AI ever tried to take over, a special command could be run that would trigger a process to wipe the operating system."

"That was a long time ago, though," said Ada.

"Right, but so the story goes, every single operating system that's been created since then still has that tiny string of code in its root directory."

"Why?"

"Who knows? Maybe some weird tradition, or maybe people are still worried about AI taking over the planet. Either way, supposedly it's still there, in everything from computers to smartphones. It's never been exploited because the command string that would trigger it was lost decades ago. The fail-safe code itself is small, but the command string to activate it is ridiculously long. In fact, it's so long, it would literally take hundreds of years to brute-force hack."

"Except this command string is saved on the Hacker's Key," guessed Ada.

"I mean, that's what people claim," said Jace. "You know, the crazy people who wear tinfoil hats because they think aliens are trying to read their minds and—" He suddenly looked uneasy. "Why are you looking so serious about this?"

"Because the Key is real," said Ada. "The United Nations had it until yesterday."

"The *United Nations*?" His eyes narrowed. *"Had?"*

"It was stolen. So I guess whoever has it now could take

down any computer network on the planet. Banks, hospitals, governments. No system is safe."

"Nah, you still don't understand," said Jace. "Assuming the person knows how to actually use it, it would be much worse than one network getting taken down."

"How much worse?" Shutting down a hospital seemed pretty bad to Ada.

"Think about it. A true, networked AI could only be destroyed if every system it was connected to was also destroyed simultaneously. So if the Root Key was designed to take down an AI, it would need to spread to every internet-enabled device instantaneously."

"Like every computer? In the world?" Ada couldn't quite believe what she was hearing.

"And every phone, every smart device, every . . . *everything*," Jace said. "Computer-guided planes falling out of the skies, world financial institutions collapsing. You name it. We'd be looking at a complete global techno-apocalypse."

"Guh . . ." Ada's brain hurt just thinking about the ramifications. The world as they knew it. Gone in an instant. She felt ill. "Yeah, that is way worse."

"How did you learn all this stuff about a real Key, anyway?" asked Jace.

"Long story. So did you finish that two-way RF device you were talking about this morning? I know my way around a command line, but network hacking is not my specialty. I might need to contact you again once I find this thing."

"No, no, no," said Jace. "It does *not* work like that. You're telling me that the Root Key exists, it has been stolen, and that you're looking for it?"

Ada nodded.

"Then I'm coming with you. There is no way I could miss out on something like this."

Ada looked at him in the dim moonlight, trying to figure out if he was serious. There was a flutter of hope in her chest at the thought that she wouldn't have to face this alone, but she fought it down. First she had to make sure he knew what he was getting into. Where it would lead. Adventures were awesome. But they usually came with a lot of risk.

"Jace . . . When I leave here, I'll have to go off the grid. Maybe forever. This place sucks, but it might be your last chance to have a normal life. If you came with me now, you'd never be able to have that."

Jace frowned. "You think I want normal? I'm offended."

"It would be *dangerous*."

"So's the neighborhood where I grew up. Look, Samus, you're definitely going to need me. And I am so tired of this place, I'm about to lose my mind."

Ada chewed on her lip. When Pascale dropped her off in

Baltimore, she'd be all alone, and she'd never been truly alone before. Not to mention, Jace was right: She probably would need him at some point. While she had a basic understanding of coding and networks, she was nowhere near as skilled or knowledgeable as he was. He had taken down half the power grid of Baltimore just to hack his previous school's network. That's what landed him at Springfield in the first place.

"Are you *sure* about this?" she asked.

"Absolutely," he said firmly.

Ada's father had always said it was important to know what skill sets a job required, to know your own limits and what you needed, and to recruit accordingly. Or maybe she was just looking for a reason to bring her best friend along. Whatever. Emotional needs were important, too.

She grinned. "Fine. But don't get mad at me when you're on the run from Interpol for the rest of your life."

"I don't even know what Interpol is, but I'm not in the habit of blaming other people for the choices I make."

"Fair enough." Her eyes narrowed as she realized they'd need a different exit strategy. "Now, how are we going to sneak you out of here, since you refuse to climb down the wall?"

"Fire codes prevent them from locking all the exits, so I think we should just go through the fire exit door like sane people."

"Won't the alarm sound?"

He shook his head. "Girl, you really are set on offending me tonight, aren't you? You don't think I worked out a bypass for those alarms on my first day here? I could have left any time. I just never had anywhere else to go."

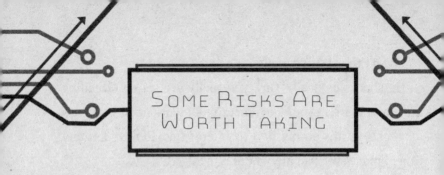

Well now, where are *you* two going?"

Jace had needed to grab a few things from his room, and now they were sneaking down the hallway back to the stairwell. But somehow they'd been caught. Not by Ms. Grand, or Mr. Albertson, or even Ms. North. No, it was much worse than that.

Ada forced a casual smile. "Hey, Cody."

Cody Francesco stood in the doorway to her room, her arms folded and her perfect face twisted into a scowl. She was normally asleep with her eye mask on by now, but tonight she was dressed in a clean uniform, her long chestnut hair carefully brushed out.

"Don't 'hey' me, empollona. What are you guys doing up past curfew?"

"Come on, Cody, be cool," pleaded Jace.

"Maybe," said Cody. "See, if it was just Frenchie here, I'd assume she was doing something weird like always. But if *you're* with her, Jace, then I know it's got to be more than that. So if you don't want me to sound the alarm, you better spill it."

Ada and Jace looked at each other, Jace with a hopeful expression, Ada with a pained one. Jace had always had a soft spot for Cody, probably because she was so poised and ladylike. She had this eerie way of getting people to do what she wanted. It was clear that Jace was already struggling not to give in to her.

"Really?" Ada asked him plaintively.

He gave her a sheepish look. "She might be able to help."

Cody's eyes narrowed. "You're escaping, aren't you?"

"Maybe," said Ada.

"Then I'm coming with you." She put her hands on her hips and nodded, as if declaring a fact.

"You think so?" asked Ada.

Cody smirked. "Jace is right. You need me."

"That's not what he said."

"Close enough." She leaned forward and gave Jace a friendly smile, like they were just casually gossiping. "So where are you going, anyway?"

He broke immediately. "Something's been stolen, and we're going to track it down."

Ada glared at him and his not-helping helpfulness. He gave her the sheepish expression again, as if that somehow excused it.

But Cody looked pleased. "So you don't know where you're going?"

"Not yet," Ada admitted.

"And it could be anywhere?" Her eyebrows raised, and there was an eager gleam in her eyes.

"I guess . . ."

"Anywhere in the *world*?"

Ada did not have patience for Cody at the best of times, and this was not even one of those times. "What's your point?"

"How many languages do you speak?"

"Five." That was stretching it. Ada's Italian was terrible.

"You speak five languages?" Jace looked impressed.

"Yeah?" cut in Cody. "Well, I speak fifteen."

Jace looked at her in awe. "You speak *fifteen* languages?"

She shrugged, like she was already bored talking about it. "I would say sixteen, except that while I can understand Swahili, I can't really speak it well. How many can you speak?"

"Do programming languages count?" asked Jace.

"Not if you can't use them to ask where the bathroom is." Cody turned back to Ada with an eager expression. "Well? Tell me that fifteen languages wouldn't be useful."

"It might," said Ada. In fact, it would be *very* useful, though she wasn't about to say that. "But not as useful as having a crew I can trust. How do I know you won't betray us the first chance you get?"

"Why *would* I?" asked Cody. "I want out of here. Not just

this school, but this country. And I'm willing to bet you already have a way of doing that."

"Possibly."

"You get me out, and I promise I'll help you find whatever it is you're looking for."

Ada knew she couldn't trust Cody's promises. But like her father always said, you *could* always trust people to do what was best for themselves.

"If you help us find what we're looking for, I'll make sure you have a passport and whatever else you need to get a fresh start somewhere else."

Cody smiled triumphantly. "It's a deal."

"Then let's get going before we're caught," said Ada. "Try to keep up."

"Hmph, more like you better not slow me down, Frenchie. I'll show you how a real world-class criminal operates. Emphasis on the *class*."

As they crept down the hallway and into the stairwell, Ada couldn't help smiling a little. It might be kind of fun to have Cody along—especially when they had to get dirty or crawl through ventilation shafts. Ada was looking forward to that a lot.

M a'am, they're heading for the exit."

A man with a square jaw and neatly parted hair sat at a desk in the guidance wing of the Springfield Military Reform School. His eyes were fixed on a monitor that showed Ada, Jace, and Cody moving cautiously down a stairwell.

"Very interesting." Ms. North watched over his shoulder, the light from the monitor glinting off her glasses.

"Should I send a squad to collect them?" asked the man.

"No, Agent West, let them go."

"Ma'am?" West turned to her, looking surprised.

"We tried it Pendleton's way, and that failed even more spectacularly than I expected. Now we do it my way."

"You think she'll actually find the Key?"

North shrugged. "Even if she doesn't, she'll at least cause enough of a stir to flush our thief out of hiding. And when he or she emerges, we'll be ready."

"Ma'am, it's just that . . ." He hesitated.

"Yes, Agent West?"

"Well, she's only a girl. She could be in a lot of danger."

"First of all, why do you all continue to underestimate

Ms. Genet after I've spoken countless times about her potential? Is it because she's not a *boy*?"

"N-no, ma'am. My apologies."

"Besides," she said, ignoring his apology, "if we don't find the Key before it's deployed, we're talking about the collapse of civilization as we know it. If the costs of preventing such a catastrophe are the lives of three juvenile delinquents, that's a sacrifice I'm willing to make. Aren't you?"

West did not look particularly happy, but he nodded. "Yes, ma'am. I suppose so."

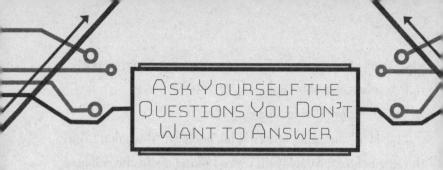

H ow did I, Pascale Benoit, the Haitian Houdini, become chauffeur to a bunch of kids?"

Pascale sighed as he drove their small gray car down the freeway that skirted Washington, DC. The evening sky flickered regularly beneath the harsh glare of evenly spaced streetlights, and the gleaming white Washington Monument shone in the distance.

"Merci beaucoup," said Ada from the passenger seat beside him. "It's not too long a drive to Baltimore, is it?"

"A couple of hours, depending on traffic," said Pascale.

"We're going to Baltimore?" asked Jace from the back seat.

"That's where my father's nearest safe house is located," said Ada.

"Hey, we could stop by my grandma's house, then."

Cody gave him a sharp look, then turned to Ada. "Is he for real?"

"We can't, Jace," Ada explained sadly. "Once they realize we're gone, the first thing they'll do is contact family and friends. I don't think you want your poor grandma interrogated by FBI agents."

"Definitely not," said Jace. "She'd have a heart attack."

"Sorry." Ada didn't know what had happened to Jace's parents, but she knew his grandmother had raised him. He was as close to her as Ada was to her father.

He sighed. "Nah, it's cool. I guess I'm still adjusting to this whole on-the-run-from-the-law thing."

"Maybe once this all blows over, we'll be able to come back."

"Speaking of which," said Cody, "since I'm going to be tagging along, I deserve to know what's actually going on. Are we on a job? If so, I want a cut."

Ada and Jace looked at each other. Again, Ada was wary and Jace was hopeful.

"We might as well tell her everything," he said.

"Yeah, I guess." Ada turned back to Cody. "Somebody stole a cyber weapon from the UN. Whoever it is, they know my dad. I have a feeling he knows who it is, but he wouldn't tell me. I think he wants me to figure it out without his help, which is cool. I just wish the stakes weren't so high."

"So once we figure out who the thief is, then what?" asked Cody.

"What do you mean?" asked Ada.

"I assume we steal this cyber weapon from them. Do you already have a buyer lined up for it?"

"Whoa, a buyer?" asked Jace.

"Why, did you want to use it yourself?" asked Cody.

"Are you kidding?" said Jace. "*Nobody* should use this thing. We should give it back to the UN so they can keep it safe. Or even better, destroy it."

"That's crazy. How would we make any money that way?" Cody looked expectantly at Ada. "Back me up here, Frenchie."

"I . . . don't know. My father didn't say what he wanted me to do with it."

"No offense, Samus, but who cares what your dad wants?" said Jace. "What do *you* want to do with it?"

Ada looked between Cody and Jace. Cody was right, of course. This whole enterprise would be dangerous and expensive. It didn't make sense to do it for free. She supposed they could try ransoming the Key to the UN, but even *if* they succeeded, was it worth suddenly being Interpol's most wanted? And the only other way to make money was to sell it to someone on the black market.

But Jace was right, too. This Key wasn't some fancy trinket for rich people. It was a dangerous weapon that was capable of harming billions of people. Could she really just sell something like that to the highest bidder? Her father was a hacker, a thief, and an outlaw, but he was not a murderer.

She couldn't imagine that he would want her to put so many people in danger.

She turned to Pascale. "What do you think we should do?"

He shook his head. "Nope, I was hired to break you out and get you to Baltimore. My responsibilities end there. You're going to have to figure this one out on your own."

Ada scowled. "Did my father tell you to say that?"

"Doesn't matter, because I agree. You can't always look to your father for the answers." He glanced at her for a moment, and his expression softened a little. "I will tell you one thing for free, though."

"What's that?"

"You're at the age now when the choices you make will decide the person you're going to become. So what kind of person do you want to be?"

Ada was a smart girl. She thought a lot about a lot of things. But she'd never really thought about that. She'd always just followed her father's lead. It hadn't always been easy, but it had always been fun. This whole year at Springfield, she'd been trying to act like she could still keep doing that, being the person she'd always been. But her father was in prison now. It sounded like he wasn't planning to escape, and they certainly weren't going to let him out for a long time. Was her old life really over? If so, what kind of new life did she want instead?

"I don't know what kind of person I want to be," she admitted.

"Well, I bet when you answer that question, you'll know what to do about the other one."

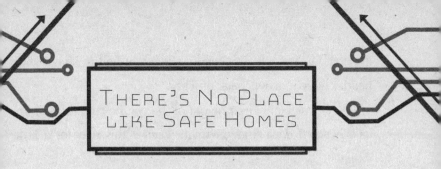

THERE'S NO PLACE
LIKE SAFE HOMES

The sky was beginning to lighten by the time they reached Baltimore. They drove past a baseball stadium, then into the downtown area, which had lots of museums, shops, and restaurants wrapped around a large harbor. The harbor was filled with all sorts of boats, from tiny sailboats to a massive old-fashioned battleship.

"Welcome to Charm City," Jace said proudly.

"It's not bad," conceded Cody.

Pascale got on another freeway, and they headed north out of the downtown area into a neighborhood called Hampden. The buildings were mostly small homes and apartment buildings, but there was a little shopping area formed by two intersecting streets that had restaurants, clothes stores, a couple of old record shops, and, most importantly, the bookstore that Ada's father had mentioned as a landmark.

Pascale pulled over across the street from Atomic Books and stopped the car without cutting the engine.

"This is where we part, chérie," he told Ada. "Good luck to all of you."

She leaned over and gave him a hug. "Thanks for

everything, Pascale. Especially since you had to shave your head. I hope it grows back quickly."

As he watched her climb out of the car, he patted his shiny bald head. "I don't know, I might keep it this way for a little while."

"You shouldn't," said Cody as she and Jace got out of the car. "Some people can pull off the bald look, but your head is kind of funny shaped in the back."

Pascale rolled his eyes, then turned to Ada. "Good luck with this one."

"Thanks," Ada said sarcastically.

"Au revoir!" He waved, then drove off.

"Huh." Jace looked around at the stores and people on their way to work.

"What is it?" asked Ada.

"This neighborhood has changed a lot. I used to come up here sometimes because there's a great record shop."

"Records?" asked Cody. "Really?"

"Don't judge me," said Jace. "I happen to like jazz. Some of the really old recordings, you can't get any other way."

"You like *jazz*? What are you, an old man?"

Jace gave Ada a pained look. "Maybe we shouldn't have brought her along after all."

"It was your idea," said Ada. "So what's changed about this neighborhood?"

He shook his head. "I don't know. There's just a lot more going on, you know? Even just a couple of years ago, there weren't this many shops and stuff."

"Is that a good thing?" she asked.

"I mean, as long as my record shop is still here . . ."

"We can look for it in a bit," said Ada. "First we have to find the safe house."

They walked to the end of the block and turned left, then another left into the alley. Across from the backs of the stores were an apartment building and the side of a church. Nestled between those two buildings was a one-story brick structure without windows. It looked like a small warehouse.

"That's it."

Ada hurried over to the door. There was a keypad instead of a traditional lock. Her father had hundreds of these little safe houses scattered all over the world. It would have been impossible to memorize a passcode for each one. But it was too risky to have the same passcode for all of them because if one was compromised, they were all compromised. So each house had its own code, but they were based on a system. Government agents were pretty clever, so it couldn't be something easy, like the street address or zip code. It had to be something that wouldn't be obvious unless you already knew the system.

Before the 1960s, phone numbers were a mixture of

numbers and letters. In smaller cities, it might have been two letters followed by three numbers, while in larger cities like New York, it might have been three letters and four numbers. Because all phone calls in those times were routed through central offices in each city, the letters came from the name of the office. For example, if a person's phone line was routed through the Harlem central office, the "number" would have been something like HAR-4247. That was the original purpose of the letters that appear beneath every digit on every phone—even modern smartphones. It was something people looked at every day but hardly ever thought about. So it was perfect for an alphanumeric translation system.

The four numbers for the keypad to each safe house came from the street name and city name of that house. But just in case a government agent knew about the old central office phone number system, Ada's father had decided to use the first and last letter of each name, rather than the first two letters, to throw them off. So the code for the safe house on Cairnes Lane in Baltimore was CSBE, or the numbers 2723.

Ada punched in the code and the light above the keypad turned green.

"We're in!"

"You sound relieved," observed Jace. "Was there some doubt?"

"No, I've just never been to this safe house before," said

Ada. "I know how the system works, but I've never done it without my dad before. Now, brace yourself. This place has probably been empty for years, so everything is going to be dusty and old."

Ada pushed open the door and flicked on the light switch. White fluorescent bulbs flickered on in the ceiling, revealing a large, open space with a cement floor. Off to one side were a desk, metal frame bunk beds, and two footlockers. Off to the other side were a small sink, a mini refrigerator, a hot plate, and a microwave. The back wall was covered by stacks of storage crates.

"Wow, you could actually live in here," said Jace as they walked into the room.

"If you *had* to," said Cody.

Ada ignored that and went over to the sink to make sure it was working. Now that she thought about it, she wondered how her father had been keeping the electricity and water on in all these safe houses while he was in prison. She decided he must have someone on the outside who did it for him.

"Oh man, is that a laptop?" Jace hurried over to the desk. "Do we have some sort of network connection here?"

"I don't know if it's working, but there should be a router and modem around somewhere," said Ada.

"I thought you said this place would be dusty," said Jace as he examined the laptop that sat on top of the desk.

"What do you mean?" asked Ada.

"There isn't a speck of dust on this desk," he said.

"That's strange . . ."

"You know what's even stranger?" Cody was crouched down in front of the mini fridge with the door open. "This fridge is on, and there's a gallon of milk in here that doesn't expire for another week."

"That can't be right . . ." Ada hurried over to the fridge, but sure enough, there was a jug of 2% milk, unopened, that wouldn't expire for six more days. "But that would mean . . ."

"Someone's been here recently," said Jace.

Suddenly the safe house didn't feel so safe. Ada looked around, her eyes scanning for anything out of place or unusual. It didn't take long to spot the box on the lower bunk bed. It was small but wrapped in brightly colored paper.

The three looked at one another.

"Is that . . ." began Cody.

"A present?" finished Jace.

Ada walked over to it slowly, her heart pounding in her chest.

"Are you sure you want to go near it?" asked Cody. "It could be, like, a *bomb* or something."

"Why do you have to say things like that?" Jace asked plaintively.

Ada stared down at the present. It was wrapped in orange

paper with yellow and red ribbons. There was a tag on it that said *For Samus*. Cody was right. It might be a bomb, or something else just as bad. But could it really be a coincidence that the name on the tag was not only her nickname, but the main character from the game cartridge that the Key's thief had left at the scene of the crime? Ada *had* to see what was inside.

Jace and Cody backed away as Ada leaned over and gently pulled the ribbons off the package. Then she carefully peeled off the tape that held the wrapping in place. She had never opened a present so slowly in her life. Her hands shook as she lifted the lid off the box.

Inside was a Geiger counter.

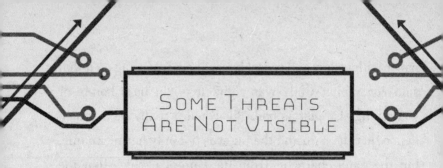

A what now?" asked Cody.

"You don't know what a Geiger counter is?" asked Jace.

She tossed her hair and looked away disdainfully. "Sorry, I'm not a gearhead like you two nerds."

"It's a device that measures radiation," said Ada.

Cody frowned. "Why would someone—"

"Oh man!" Jace looked panicked. "Did someone irradiate this place? Quick, turn it on!"

Ada switched on the device, and all three of them huddled around it.

"Radiation is bad, right?" Cody asked nervously. "Like *kill you* bad?"

"First, you start throwing up all over the place." Jace's face was tense.

"Ew," said Cody.

Jace continued. "Then you get sores all over your body."

"Gross," said Cody.

"Then your hair falls out."

"You're kidding."

"Then you start bleeding out of *everywhere*, even your butt."

"I can't even . . ." Cody looked like she was ready to faint.

"And *then* you die," said Jace.

"Well, what does the counter thingy say?" demanded Cody.

"Nothing," said Ada. "There's no radiation here."

Jace let out a huge sigh. "I can't tell you . . . radiation sickness is one of my worst nightmares. It's right up there with clowns."

Ada frowned at the Geiger counter, then at the packaging that still lay on the bunk.

"Frenchie doesn't seem relieved," Cody observed.

"Why would I be?" asked Ada. "*Somebody* other than me and my father broke into one of our safe houses. How did they do that? And why would they leave a Geiger counter specifically for me, if there isn't any radiation here?"

"And a gallon of milk," said Jace.

"Yeah, that might be even weirder," said Ada. "Who breaks into a secure location and leaves an unopened jug of milk?"

Cody shrugged. "Who knows? Anyway, do you think stores are open yet? Because I have *got* to get out of this school uniform."

Ada gestured to the crates in the back of the room. "We have clothes here. There should be stuff that would fit you."

Cody's eyes narrowed as she assessed Ada's black-and-gray outfit. "No offense, but Urban Ninja isn't really my look."

Ada sighed and reached into her duffel bag. She tossed Cody a stack of bills. "Fine, but don't buy too much. We need to travel light."

Cody grinned as she caught the money. "For real? Hey, maybe you're not so bad after all, Frenchie."

"Why do you call me that?" asked Ada. "I haven't lived in France any longer than anywhere else, and my mom was American."

"Your English is fine, I guess, but you speak Spanish with a French accent."

Ada's eyes widened in outrage. "I do not!"

"You really do, but it's fine. I'm here to make up for your poor language skills. Anyway, I'm off to see what kind of fashion Charm City has to offer, so chao."

Cody spun on her heel, swirling her hair as she did, and left. Once she was gone, Ada gave Jace a long look.

"What?" He already seemed a little guilty.

"You know."

He sighed. "We had to bring her along. She would have raised the alarm, and then we would have been stuck in Springfield and probably moved into C Class."

"You *wanted* her along. Do you like her or something?"

"What? No!" His eyes darted around, looking everywhere

but at Ada, and he started fiddling with his sleeve. "That's ridiculous."

"Hmm."

"I don't," he insisted. "Not like you're thinking."

Ada didn't buy it. She decided she couldn't trust Jace's opinion when it came to Cody. Hopefully it wouldn't become a problem.

"*Anyway*," said Jace, clearly wanting to change the subject. "What do you think the point of the Geiger counter is?"

"I think whoever broke in here knows me and my dad. They left my nickname on the package. And whoever stole the Key also left a present for my dad with his name on it. I think it's the same person."

"So what, they're leaving you clues on how to catch them, supervillain style?"

"I honestly don't know." She put the Geiger counter down on the desk and started searching the drawers for the old address book with local contacts her father kept at each safe house. "Before we worry about any of that, I need to get you and Cody passports."

"We leaving the country?"

"Agent Pendleton said the Key was stolen from an island off the coast of Iceland, so I guess we start there." She found the small bound book and flipped to the *F*s, for *forgers*. She found a name and local number listed. She'd been a little worried that Baltimore might not have one, since it wasn't a big city. But maybe any city that had direct international flights would have at least one reliable passport forger.

"Iceland, huh?" Jace did not look excited. "Gonna be cold?"

"Probably. We should have coats in storage, or I can give you money to go buy stuff like Cody." She looked around for the burner phone—a prepaid, untraceable cell phone she could use to call the passport forger.

"Hey, Ada?"

"Hm?" Ada found the burner phone on a charger stand in the kitchen area. It was just a cheap plastic flip phone. Probably a couple of years old at least, but it seemed to work fine.

"Earlier, you said your mom *was* American." Jace sat on the lower bunk, looking at her with a serious expression. "She dead?"

Ada looked down at the flip phone. His expression made her a little uncomfortable. Not that he was being pushy or anything. He was just interested. But this wasn't a topic she liked to talk about. In fact, if Cody was still there, she probably wouldn't have said anything. Since it was just Jace, though, she thought maybe he would understand.

"I don't know what happened to my mom. Maybe she's dead, or in prison, or she could just be out there somewhere in the world doing her own thing. She left us when I was five, and my dad doesn't talk about her."

"Oh," said Jace.

After a few moments of silence, Ada asked, "What about your parents?"

"My mom died in Afghanistan."

"She was a soldier?"

He nodded, looking proud. "Marine."

"What about your dad?"

"I never met him."

"Oh."

He smiled, although it looked a little forced. "It's not so bad, really. You can't miss someone you never met, right?"

"Yeah, I guess . . ." Ada wasn't so sure about that, but it seemed like Jace wanted her to agree with him.

"Do you miss your mom?" he asked her.

Ada thought about it for a moment, then shook her head. "Honestly, I don't remember her too well. But in all the memories I *do* have of Lilith Genet, she was terrifying."

It took three days, but the fake passports for Jace and Cody were finally ready. Even Cody had to admit they looked great. The afternoon the passports arrived, Ada and her friends packed up their few belongings, including coats and the mysterious Geiger counter, and took the bus straight to the airport.

BWI was fairly small compared to the airports in places like New York, London, and Paris, and the international wing was even smaller. That made it easy to find their way around. Ada paid in cash for three one-way tickets at the Iceland Air counter, and they headed toward the security check. That was when Ada realized the downside to it being a smaller airport. It was difficult to hide in the crowd. And that was a problem because there were two FBI agents posted at the metal detector.

"Frenchie, are you seeing this?" Cody muttered as they got into the security line.

"Yep."

"I'm not seeing it," said Jace. "Care to fill me in?"

"Two men at the security check in black suits and

earpieces with suspicious gun-sized bulges in their jackets," said Cody.

"But our names are different on these passports, and we're not in school uniforms anymore." Jace had opted to buy new clothes as well and now wore jeans, sneakers, and a purple Baltimore Ravens hoodie. Cody was in a dress, even though Ada had reminded her they were going to Iceland. "Will they really be able to recognize our faces?"

"Ms. North will have given them our school ID photos by now," said Ada.

"Oh man, that's right. So what are we going to *do*?"

Jace looked panicked. At first Ada felt frustrated that he was getting rattled already. But she reminded herself how new all this was for him. He'd never even flown in an airplane before, and already he had to worry about getting collared by FBI agents. When she thought about it from his perspective, she realized he was actually being really cool about it all.

"Maybe we should get out of line," said Cody.

"No, that would draw attention to us," said Ada.

"Then *what*?" asked Jace.

"I'm thinking . . ."

Then a male voice directly behind her spoke in Russian. "Excuse me, miss. Might I be of some assistance?"

Ada glanced back sharply and saw a familiar face.

"Shukhov!"

The short, bald Russian agent nodded politely beneath his round fur hat. "Ms. Genet, how nice to see you again."

"Who's *this* guy?" Jace asked suspiciously.

"He knows Ada," Cody said, though with no less suspicion.

"He was with the other agents where my father was being interrogated," said Ada.

Shukhov gave her a pained look. "I did not agree with Pendleton's plan any more than your Ms. North did, but there was little I could do. At least there. Here, I might be much more useful to you."

Ada's eyes narrowed. "How so?"

"You need to escape the notice of those FBI agents, correct? If you allow me to go in front of you, I can keep them occupied while you go through the regular security check."

"And in return?"

Shukhov gave her a faint smile. "Let's just say I owe your father a few favors."

Ada and her father had done a number of jobs for the Russians over the years, so it wasn't too difficult to believe. Besides, she wasn't sure how else they'd get past.

"Fine. But if you cross us, I have no problem implicating you as an accomplice in my escape. Perhaps even the mastermind."

He chuckled lightly. "As wary as your father, I see. Very

well, this will give me the opportunity to prove that I can be a valuable ally to you."

Ada stepped aside so the Russian agent could get in front of them.

"What just happened?" asked Jace.

Cody gave Ada a thoughtful look as she spoke. "That Russian is going to cause a distraction so we can get past the FBI agents."

"And *why* is he doing that?"

"Unclear," said Cody.

"He said he owes my father," said Ada.

"I heard him," said Cody. "I just don't know if I believe him."

"Oh, I definitely don't," said Ada. "But if it doesn't work, we'll be no worse off."

"Not true," said Jace. "If it doesn't work, we'll already be up there at the scanner instead of hiding in a line, and at that point we won't have any other options."

"Okay, yeah," admitted Ada. "But do either of you have a better plan?"

The two looked at each other.

"I didn't think so," said Ada. "Besides, while I don't think we can trust Shukhov, I *do* think we can trust that he doesn't want us to get caught by the US government. We might as well use that to our advantage."

Standing in the security line at an airport was never fun, but as they slowly made their way toward the two FBI agents, the wait was excruciating. At long last, they piled their bags, coats, and shoes onto the conveyor belt and moved to the line for the scanner.

Shukhov was directly in front of them and went first. He stepped into the clear glass scanning booth and lifted his arms over his head. As the scanner swept past him, alarms started going off. Suddenly guards were everywhere, and the FBI agents were swept up with them as they pulled Shukhov out of the scanning booth and began to pat him down. They found a small gun and Shukhov began speaking very apologetically in Russian about how he was a foreign diplomat and that he may have forgotten to remove a few items from his pockets. Of course, none of the guards spoke Russian, so they had no idea what he was saying. The FBI agents started to question him, and he replied in an exaggerated broken English that was barely intelligible. The agents did catch the word *diplomat*, so they began making calls to see if his claims checked out.

During the commotion, the regular TSA agents were still bringing people through the scanner. The FBI didn't even glance in Ada's direction as she patiently stood with her arms over her head inside the scanning booth. All three of them were already past the checkpoint and putting their shoes back on when Shukhov was taken away by the FBI agents for questioning.

"What did I tell you?" Ada said smugly.

"I guess you were right," said Jace.

"Hm" was all Cody said.

Ada was pretty sure Cody was just having trouble admitting she'd been wrong.

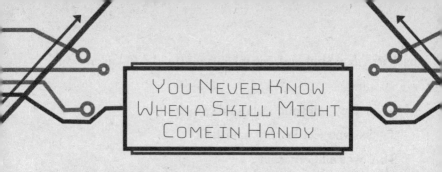

The flight from Baltimore to Iceland took about six hours. Keflavík Airport was small but crowded. For many years, Iceland's tourism bureau had pitched the country as a perfect stopover point between North America and continental Europe, since it was between them. Magazines in the airplane and posters in the airport urged people to take an extra day or two during their journey to stop and enjoy all the wonders Iceland had to offer, which included geysers, hot springs, and the northern lights.

Since it was spring, however, between the northern lights viewing in the winter and the relative warmth of summer, not a lot of people seemed to be stopping. Instead, travelers rushed from one gate to another, hurrying in all directions toward their next destination. Other people sat in chairs in common areas eating a snack or drinking a beverage as they waited for a connecting flight. Overhead announcements were made in the light, skittering Icelandic language, followed by the English translation.

Ada and her friends stood in the middle of the endless

flowing streams of people and looked around them in a jet-lagged daze. It was seven in the morning in Iceland, but it was still only three in the morning in Baltimore. They had tried to sleep a few hours on the plane, but even so, their bodies hadn't adjusted yet.

"So . . . we're in Iceland," said Jace. "What now?"

"We should probably go to Reykjavík, the capital," said Ada, "then hire a boat to take us out to the island where the Key was stolen."

"And how to we get to Reka . . . Reka . . ." Jace gave up on pronouncing the name. "To the capital?"

"Let me ask," said Cody.

Ada and Jace watched as Cody strolled confidently over to a large man with a red beard and began talking to him. After a few minutes, she came back, looking pleased with herself.

"There's a bus. Follow me, I know where we catch it."

"I can't believe you speak Icelandic," said Ada.

"Fifteen languages, remember?" Cody said over her shoulder as she began to walk quickly through the airport.

Ada and Jace hurried to catch up with her.

"Yeah but, *Icelandic*? How often does it actually come in handy?"

"Hardly ever," admitted Cody. "I just learned it because I

like it. It's such a gentle, flowing language. Speaking Icelandic feels like a babbling brook trickling over your tongue."

"Cody, you are a lot weirder than I realized," said Jace.

"Coming from you, I'll take that as a compliment," she said.

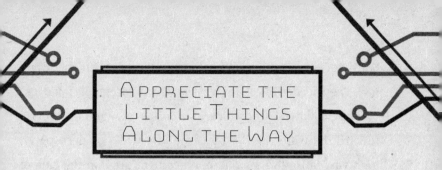

The bus took Ada and her friends across the flat Icelandic landscape. The winter snow had melted, revealing rocks and grass that hadn't turned green yet. There were hardly any trees or shrubbery, giving the stony brown fields a desolate appearance.

It took about an hour to reach Reykjavík. The city was larger in size than Baltimore but had a smaller population, so its narrow cobblestone streets were quiet, and only a few people walked past. The buildings in the downtown area were nonetheless packed in tightly together, often painted in gentle pastel greens, yellows, or pinks.

"Okay," said Cody as they filed out of the bus and onto the sidewalk. "Before we find a boat, I'm going to insist we go to Bæjarins Beztu."

"The what now?" asked Jace.

"*Bæjarins beztu pylsur,*" said Cody. "The best hot dogs in town."

"Hot dogs?" Jace asked warily. "In Iceland?"

"Trust me."

Jace looked questioningly at Ada, but she only shrugged.

She'd never been to Iceland before, and it was clear that Cody had. They needed to eat anyway, so why not Icelandic hot dogs?

They followed Cody down a series of winding streets toward the water until they came to a wide, modern paved highway. Sitting in a small open cement area on the side of the highway was a tiny red-and-white building. It was really more of a booth, with a few picnic tables beside it.

"*This* is the best hot dog place in Iceland?" Jace didn't look convinced.

Cody smirked. "Just you wait."

Ada gave her some of the Icelandic money she had exchanged at the airport and then sat down at one of the picnic tables while Cody ordered at the booth.

Jace sat down beside Ada. "My first meal in a foreign country is going to be hot dogs."

"You wanted something more exotic?" she asked. "I bet we can find a place that serves traditional Icelandic foods, like sheep's head or fermented shark."

"Yeah, um, no thanks. I'm good." He leaned in and said more quietly, "Have you noticed there are like zero black people here?"

"No Asians or Latinx, either," said Cody as she sat down across from them with three hot dogs.

"Hey, yeah," said Jace. "Everybody here looks like they could be Ada's sister, right?"

"What does *that* mean?" asked Ada.

"Pale, thin, and blond describes like three-fourths of the population of Iceland." Cody shrugged. "It's a small, isolated island country, so it's just not going to be as diverse as a huge place like the US."

She handed them each a hot dog. "Verði þér að góðu. That means 'enjoy your meal.'"

Jace stared down at his hot dog, which had a strip of brown sauce and a strip of white sauce running across it. "Uh, what's on this?"

"Mashed puffin brains," said Cody.

Jace stared at her in horror.

She laughed. "Kidding. The brown stuff is sweet mustard. The white stuff is called remolaði. It's like a funky mayonnaise. Just try it."

Ada and Cody watched expectantly as Jace slowly bit down on his hot dog. His expression became almost contemplative as he chewed and swallowed.

"That . . . is so strange."

Cody grinned. "Right?"

"It's *like* a hot dog . . . but not. I don't know what else to say."

"I *think* you're supposed to say, 'Thank you for taking me to this amazing food stall, Cody. I will always trust your dining recommendations forever,'" said Cody.

Ada bit down on her hot dog and even she had to admit that Cody was right. It was delicious.

Sometimes, Ada had a habit of getting focused on a task and ignoring everything else. Her father had to constantly remind her that it was important to notice all the supposedly "unimportant" stuff along the way. After all, what was the point of being in a new country if you didn't take the time to appreciate it? Maybe she still needed to be reminded of that now and then.

"I guess I'm glad we brought you along after all," she told Cody.

"Because of the hot dogs?" Cody looked surprised.

"And other things," said Ada. "But the hot dogs sealed it."

The smile that Cody gave her was unexpectedly shy. Ada hadn't thought Cody really cared whether they wanted her along or not. Maybe Ms. Fifteen Languages and Perfect Hair wasn't quite as arrogant as she sometimes seemed.

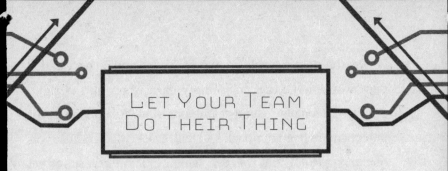

LET YOUR TEAM
DO THEIR THING

Once Ada and her friends finished their Icelandic hot dogs, they walked over to the docks. They found a guy with a small powerboat who agreed to take them out. The guy had long blond hair and looked kind of like an older version of Thor from the movies. He didn't speak much English, so the negotiations were done by Cody in Icelandic.

Once Cody and the captain had settled on a price, they set out on the rippling black waters in the speedy little boat. It hadn't been too cold in Reykjavík, but out on the water, the wind made it feel a lot colder. All three of them pulled jackets out of their travel packs, and Cody also put on a round fur hat.

The boat hugged the coast until it rounded the Reykjanes Peninsula, then turned south into open waters.

Cody had to shout over the roar of the engine. "I told Captain Briem what we're looking for. He says there's a small group of islands southeast of the mainland, and he's seen a couple of helicopters coming and going from one of them for the last few days."

"I bet that's it," said Ada.

For the next few hours, the rocky Icelandic coast glided past on the left, with only empty dark water on the right. Finally the smaller islands came into view. Ada pulled a pair of binoculars from her pack and took a closer look. There was one in particular that was even smaller than the rest and set a little ways apart. The island was so tiny and unremarkable that Ada might not have even noticed it, except there were two large black helicopters parked next to a solitary shack.

"That's got to be it." She handed the binoculars to Jace and pointed out the island.

"With those four government-looking dudes in suits walking around, I'd say so."

"Yeah, I guess there's no point in trying to keep it a secret now."

"What do you think they're doing?" asked Jace.

"Probably looking for clues, just like us."

"And what makes you think we'll find something they won't?"

Ada gave him an offended look. "I spent most of my childhood evading people like this. They all think too much like government agents and not enough like a thief. Trust me, I'll see possibilities they haven't even imagined."

"Okay, but how are we going to get past them all?" asked Jace. "I doubt they'll just let a couple of random kids look around."

"Let me see." Cody held out her hand, and Jace gave her the binoculars. She examined the island for a few moments, then smiled. "Oh yeah, I got this."

"How?" asked Jace.

"I'll cause a distraction to lure them all away from the shack, and then you and Ada sneak over to look for clues." Cody turned to Ada. "I hope we still have plenty of money. I'll need Captain Briem's help, and that'll probably cost us."

"We've got money, but are you *sure* you can do this?" asked Ada.

"I may not be able to climb buildings, escape prisons, or hack computer systems, but I can definitely distract a few macho government agents. Forget about the hot dogs, let me show you the *real* reason you should be glad to have me along."

Ada still wasn't sure she could trust Cody, but maybe that was because she hadn't given her a chance to prove herself.

"Fine. It's your show. What do you need us to do?"

ody had to do some fast talking in Icelandic and wave around a bunch of money before Captain Briem finally agreed to what she wanted. Then he took the boat around to the side of the island where the view from the helicopters would be blocked by the shack.

There was a small dinghy tied up to the back of the boat. Ada and Jace eased it into the water, then climbed aboard. Once they were settled, Ada waved to the captain. He nodded and steered the larger boat forward, continuing to the other side of the island with Cody still aboard.

The dinghy was just a small fiberglass boat that barely fit the two of them. It didn't even have an outboard motor, just a pair of oars. They didn't have far to row, but the water was so choppy it took nearly ten minutes before the dinghy's bottom scraped the black sand of the beach.

"Whew," said Jace as they climbed out. "That is a lot harder than it looks."

They dragged the dinghy all the way out of the water so

it didn't get taken away by the tide, then sat down on the cold sand to wait for Cody's signal.

"I guess you're starting to trust her more?" asked Jace.

"We'll see," said Ada.

"You mean if this goes well, you will trust her?"

"I'll trust that she has her uses, anyway," said Ada.

"You know what I think? You two are rivals. Like Goku and Vegeta."

"What's a goku?"

Jace looked shocked. "Do you not know *Dragon Ball*?"

Ada shook her head.

"It's like the best fighting anime ever made. When this is over, you and I will have to watch, like, *all of it*. Except *GT*. Nobody should watch that."

When this is over . . . Ada didn't know where she'd be, or what she'd be doing, when this was over. Could she go back to Springfield? Did she want to? If not, would she just travel around the world, trying to hustle jobs like she and her father used to do? But she'd have to do it alone now, and that didn't sound like nearly as much fun.

Meanwhile, Jace was still going on about his whole "rivals" idea.

"Yeah. You two are definitely rivals. Sure, you don't really get along, but you respect each other's skills and you challenge each other to be better."

"I'm not sure I respect Cody's skills."

"You seemed pretty impressed that she can speak fifteen languages."

"I suppose."

"And if she pulls this off?"

"Then I guess she's *somewhat* useful."

Jace smiled with satisfaction. "Spoken like a true rival."

Then there was a shrill scream from the other side of the island.

"That's the signal." Ada pulled out the binoculars and edged around the back of the shack until she could see their boat. It was less than ten feet from the shore, which was a little close for comfort in such shallow waters. Cody had jumped down into the water and was now splashing loudly and hysterically toward shore. Ada winced. That had to be really cold.

The agents all turned toward the commotion as Cody staggered out of the water. She was speaking in Icelandic, but even if the agents didn't speak the language, her panic was unmistakable. They hurried over to her and tried to calm her down.

"Let's move," said Ada.

She and Jace circled around the far side of the shack as Cody fed the agents a story about her poor "papa" passing out in the boat and could they please come help him. It was a classic damsel-in-distress routine. So classic, in fact, that Ada was amazed that the agents were falling for it.

"That girl could be a movie actress," said Jace as they crept toward the front door. "I halfway believe her and I *know* it's not true."

Ada had to admit he was right. Cody was sobbing, her voice shaking as she spoke in broken English. She looked truly terrified. Maybe all it took to breathe life into the classics was a convincing performance.

Ada didn't have time to ponder it too much. Cody said she'd only have about ten minutes, so she had to make the most of it.

First was the front door.

"Is that a magnetic lock?" asked Jace.

Ada nodded. "Impossible to pick."

"Maybe they stole someone's key?"

"The easier thing to do is just wait until someone comes out. The guards had to be on some sort of schedule. You observe them for a few days and figure out what it is."

"Okay, but how would anyone be able to observe this place for a few days without being seen?" asked Jace. "There is literally nothing around this shack but sand and ocean."

"Hmm. Good point. Not sure yet, but we have to keep moving."

Once they were inside, the shack was nice but not fancy. There were a couple of beds and a tiny kitchen. And two chalk body outlines on the floor.

"The guards?" asked Jace.

"Probably."

Jace stared at the white outlines for a moment. "When you and your dad did stuff like this, did you ever . . . you know, kill anyone?"

"Absolutely not. My father would never kill anyone."

Jace looked relieved. "Okay, cool. I mean, as much as I love hacking into stuff, when I shut down that power grid in Baltimore . . . I didn't even think about it at the time, but there was a hospital in there."

"Hospitals have backup generators, don't they?"

"Yeah, and everyone was fine. But what if the generator had failed? I might have killed people, you know? And I just . . ." He stared down at the chalk outlines like they were his own victims.

Ada touched his shoulder. "It's okay, Jace. I get why it bothers you. But that didn't happen. Nobody died because of you. And now you know better. So don't beat yourself up about it."

Jace shook himself, like he was coming out of a dream. "Yeah, thanks, Samus. Okay, what's next?"

"Trapdoor." Ada knelt next to the open door and examined

the lock system. "Ugh, retinal scanning? What decade is this?"

"I thought biometrics like that were pretty reliable," said Jace.

"All you need is a printout of the person's eye."

"You're kidding."

"Nope. The retina image needs to be a minimum of seventy-five pixels and the print needs to be at least twelve hundred dpi. If you have that, the scanner is fooled."

"Okay, but that's pretty hi-res. Like, you would have to be all up in there taking that picture of someone's eye. How would they do that without being suspicious?"

"Maybe the picture already existed," said Ada. "Or our thief could have hacked a retinal database and gotten it from there."

"Just so long as they didn't pull somebody's eye out to do it."

"That only happens in movies," Ada assured him. "In reality, if someone tried to pluck an eye out, it would be hard to keep it intact. Even if they did, the eyeball would start decomposing pretty quickly. Of course they could put the eye on ice to slow decomposition, but the freezing temperatures might warp the retina in a way that would make it fail the scan . . ."

Ada noticed Jace's horrified expression and cleared her

throat, feeling her face flush with embarrassment. Sometimes she got so caught up in the logistics of figuring out how something was done that she forgot they were still talking about actual humans.

"Anyway, let's go down."

"Yeah . . ." said Jace, still looking a little unnerved.

The hatch led down into a small bunker with a door at the end. Ada noticed vents in the cement walls. Some sort of poison gas defense? There was a microphone next to the door.

"Voice recognition," she said wearily.

"Don't tell me, all they'd need is a recording of the person speaking the passphrase."

"Worse, all they'd need is enough recordings of the person that they could splice the passphrase together from different tracks."

"That still doesn't explain how the thief learned the passphrase in the first place."

"True."

On the other side of the door was a small, bulletproof glass case with a thumbprint scanning system.

"Okay, even *I* know that a thumbprint scan can be faked," said Jace. "Didn't some dude in Japan do it with a gummy bear once?"

"His name is Tsutomu Matsumoto," Ada said absently.

"And it was homemade gelatin, but yeah, basically the same thing."

Ada was far more interested in what was inside the case. The old *Metroid* game cartridge Agent Pendleton had mentioned was still in there. *For Remy* was written on it in black marker.

"Huh . . ." she said.

"You got something?" Jace asked eagerly.

"I just . . . that handwriting looks familiar, but I can't place it."

"Well, you said it's someone your dad knows, so you've probably seen it before."

"Yeah. I just wish I could connect it with *who*. My dad knows a *lot* of people capable of doing this."

They stared at the case for a few moments.

"So how about those special clues you were going to notice?" asked Jace. "You know, while you're thinking like a thief."

"Very funny."

"Mind if I try something?" he asked.

"Be my guest."

Jace opened up his pack and took out the Geiger counter.

"Why did you bring that along?"

"It has to mean something, right? Someone went to a lot of trouble to get it to us. It's been bothering me." He switched the counter on. When he held it next to the *Metroid* cartridge, the needle on the dial bounced and the device began clicking. It showed trace amounts of radiation. Nothing harmful. In fact, it was barely measurable. But it was there.

"Oh man, I think I know what happened!" said Jace.

"Tell me," said Ada.

"Okay . . ." Jace held the counter up to the door handle, and the needle gave another tiny jump. "Yeah, this is . . ." He held it up to the ladder and the counter registered a trace amount of radiation there as well. "Ho, man, I really got it!"

"Jace, Come on!"

"Sorry, sorry. Follow me."

Jace climbed back up to ground level and Ada followed. He pointed to the front door with the magnetic lock.

"I was thinking . . . How would they spy on the guards to learn their schedule?"

"Right. Like you said, they had nowhere to hide."

"Yeah, that's what I meant, but what I actually *said* was 'nothing but sand and water.' And see, you can hide in water."

"It would be too cold for an extended stakeout. Even in a wetsuit."

"Yeah, but not in a submarine."

Ada stared at him as she realized what he was saying. "The trace radiation is coming from someone who's spent a lot of time near the reactor of a nuclear-powered sub."

"While that person was spying on the guards with a periscope."

"And that's how they got here and how they got away without being detected. They used a submarine." Ada frowned. "Which are impossible to track."

Jace grinned at her. "Oh, I wouldn't say *impossible* . . ."

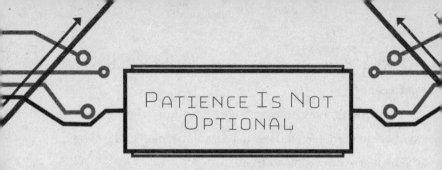

Ada and Jace snuck back to the dinghy with minutes to spare. They peeked from behind the shack to watch the agents return to their posts, all looking very pleased with themselves, clearly thinking they'd saved Cody's "father." Captain Briem must have given a pretty convincing performance of unconsciousness, as well.

The boat engines started up. Captain Briem took a wide circle to the back of the island, so it wasn't obvious that he was coming around to get Ada and Jace.

Once they were back on board, Cody gave them an expectant look. "Well? I hope it was worth it."

Ada looked at Jace. "Was it?"

Jace nodded. "Just get me somewhere with internet, and I should be able to figure out which way the sub was heading."

Cody's eyes widened. "They escaped by submarine?"

"Looks like it," said Ada.

"And how did you figure that out?"

"The Geiger counter picked up trace amounts of radiation left behind, which—"

"Okay, you're about to launch into a nerd speech," said Cody. "I am freezing cold and not in the mood, so let's just skip it and say I trust you."

They were quiet as Captain Briem took them back along the coast to Reykjavík. The sun broke through the lead gray clouds for a little while, turning the sea to a dark bluish green. But it didn't do much to warm them up. Poor Cody was still wet and shivering, so Jace gave her his coat to wear on top of her own.

They finally made it to the capital around sunset and found a youth hostel to spend the night. Ada hadn't been in a hostel in a while; they were actually a lot like the accommodations at Springfield Military Reform School: tiny rooms with bunk beds, shared bathrooms, and a common kitchen and living room area. Of course, they lacked the guards, hall monitors, and secret agents, so it was definitely an improvement.

The hostel also had a few computers in the common area.

"Will this work?" asked Ada.

Jace eyed up the ancient, wheezing PCs. His eyes gleamed with eagerness and he wiggled his fingers. "It'll do just fine."

"What is it you're going to do exactly?" asked Cody.

Jace sat down at a computer and opened a command terminal as he spoke. "You know China basically has their own internet, right?"

"I guess I heard something about that," said Cody. "It's like the rest of the world's, but separate?"

"Not exactly like the rest of the world's, because everything in it is controlled by the Chinese government," said Jace. "And not totally separate. At least not if you're really, *really* good at intrusion."

"Like you," said Ada.

Jace beamed. "Exactly."

"But how does that help us?" asked Cody.

Jace's fingers raced across the keyboard as he began to issue commands from the terminal. "I won't bore you with a lecture about firewalls, proxy filters, VPNs—"

"Thank you," said Cody.

Jace looked disappointed. Maybe he'd wanted to talk about those things at least a *little*. But he nodded. "The bottom line is that on the other side of China's Great Firewall, the government has a lot of surveillance tech that they don't share with the rest of the world. For example, a satellite system that uses lasers to locate submarines."

"Lasers?" asked Cody.

"Not the *Star Wars* blow-things-up kind of lasers," said Jace. "These are intense beams of light that project down into the ocean. When they hit something like a coral reef or a submarine, they bounce back to the satellite in a series of pulses that computers can interpret into objects."

"So it uses light to locate things the same way a bat uses sound?" asked Ada.

"Basically, yeah. Submarines also give off a crazy amount of heat because of their nuclear reactors. That disperses pretty quickly when the sub is more than a hundred meters down, but to spy on those guards, ours would have been pretty close to the surface for at least a few days. So first we find their heat signature, and then we use data from the laser system to see which way they went."

"And?" Cody's eyes were wide as she stared at the computer screen. "Have you found it?"

Jace paused in his typing and looked over his shoulder at her. "You cannot rush something like this. Unless you want the Chinese government knocking on the door of this hostel before morning."

"Um, no thanks," said Cody.

"I have to be careful and make sure I cover my tracks. That takes time."

"Sorry. I won't rush you."

Ada understood Cody's impatience, but she also knew enough about hacking and coding to know that Jace's skills were way beyond her. There was nothing she could do to help.

"Let's leave Jace alone and go find some food," she suggested.

"Just bring me something back." Jace's hands flashed across the keyboard with dizzying speed.

"Sheep head or fermented shark?" asked Ada.

"Ha" was all he said, his eyes still locked on the screen.

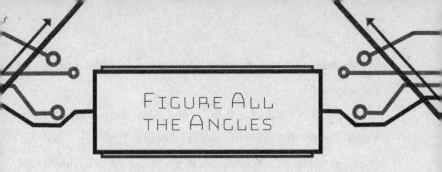

The streets of Reykjavík were empty after dark. Ada wondered if that was because it was between tourist seasons, or if people didn't go out much. She could hear music coming out of a bar as they walked past, and a few restaurants were still open, but otherwise it was quiet.

"So . . ." said Cody. "I've been thinking about that Geiger counter thing."

"What about it?" Ada hoped she didn't have to explain how it worked. She didn't think she could do it in a way that Cody would understand.

But Cody was thinking about it differently. "Would Jace have realized we were looking for a submarine without that counter?"

"I don't know. Maybe not."

"So whoever gave it to you wanted you to figure it out. But who?"

"Not the thief," said Ada. "No real thief would give clues on how to catch them."

"Probably not the US government, either," said Cody. "If they wanted to help you, they wouldn't be trying to catch us.

What about that Russian guy, Shukhov, who helped us out at the airport?"

"I guess it could be him," said Ada. "But if he already knew about the sub, he could probably track it, too. An army of Russian hackers could do what Jace is doing. So why bother with us?" She frowned. "Although we still don't know the real reason why he even bothered to help us in the first place."

"So you see where I'm going with this, right?" asked Cody. "Why is *anyone* helping us? What do they have to gain?"

Once again Ada was surprised and, she had to admit, a little impressed. Cody might not know a lot about technology, but she knew people. She understood how they worked. Ada thought about what Jace had said about them being rivals who challenged each other to grow. Maybe there was something to that after all.

"I don't know what anyone could gain by helping us find the Key rather than just go after it themselves," Ada admitted.

"Me either," said Cody. "And I don't like when I can't figure all the angles. Smells like a setup."

"But that's just like the help question," said Ada. "Who would set us up, and why?"

"I don't know, but there's a big chunk of this that we're missing right now."

They picked up three orders of fish and chips and brought it back to the hostel, where they found Jace waiting for them, his eyes wide with excitement.

"I got it!" he said as they sat down at one of the large common tables in the kitchen.

"You found the sub?" Ada bit down on a big piece of fried fish. It was a lot lighter and flakier than the British version.

"Yup." Jace shoveled several of the thick chips—or fries, as he would have called them—into his mouth before continuing. Then he leaned back and sighed. "Man, I was hungry."

"So?" pressed Cody. "Where did it go?"

"Well, that's the part I'm not sure about," said Jace. "It headed southeast. I lost it for a while in the Atlantic, but I followed its trajectory and picked it up again off the western coast of Ireland. It must have been pretty close to the surface because there was a massive heat signature that went right up to the coast. Then it just . . . disappeared."

"Disappeared?" asked Cody.

"That's what it looked like."

"What if it just turned off its reactor when it got to the coast?" asked Ada.

Jace shook his head. "Nah, then the heat would have gradually dissipated. This was sudden. It was there, and then it was gone."

"So it found a way to shield itself?" asked Cody.

"No idea how, but yeah," said Jace.

Ada frowned. "Where on the Irish coast did it disappear?"

"I don't know Ireland very well. On the map it looked like a stretch of coast between two towns, Doolin and Liscannor."

Ada's eyes widened. "The Cliffs of Moher."

"What's that?" asked Jace.

"Our next destination," said Ada.

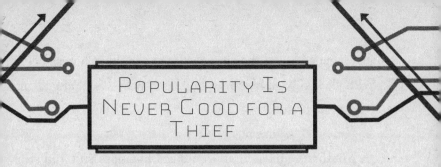

The flight from Keflavík to Dublin was about two and a half hours, and there was only a one-hour time difference, so that part of the trip wasn't too bad. But unfortunately, they still had a long way to go before they reached the Cliffs of Moher. First they would need to take a bus from the airport to the Dublin train station. Then they would need to take the train for another two and a half hours across Ireland to Galway. From there, they would need to take a bus to the cliffs.

They stocked up on snacks at the overpriced airport grocery, then headed to the bus stop that would take them to the train station.

"I can't believe the Irish put potato chips *inside* sandwiches," said Jace as he happily munched away. "I also can't believe nobody else thought of it."

"Just wait until you have a full Irish breakfast," said Cody. "I think we'll have time for one, right, Ada?"

"Yeah, we'll probably have to spend the night at a hostel in Galway, then head to the cliffs tomorrow . . ."

Ada's voice trailed away as she stared at a man who had

just stepped out of the airport. It was the thin Chinese agent with slicked-back hair who had been with Ms. Wang at the supermax prison.

"Guys . . ." Ada said.

Another Chinese man in a black business suit and sunglasses appeared, and the two began talking, their faces grim.

It didn't look like they'd spotted Ada yet, but the bus wouldn't be coming for another ten minutes or so, and that was much too long to be standing out in the open.

"You know what, guys, let's splurge on a taxi," Ada said brightly as she ushered them over to the taxi queue.

"You don't have to tell me twice," Cody said enthusiastically. "Honestly, I hate buses."

"I thought you said we had to be careful about money," said Jace.

Ada positioned herself so that she was hidden behind Jace, who thankfully was taller and broader than her.

"Don't turn around," she muttered, "but I think there are Chinese government agents over there. I assume they're after *us*."

"*What?*" Jace's head twitched, like he had to fight not to look.

"Nice going, leet haxor," Cody said.

"No, it couldn't be my fault," said Jace. "I covered my

tracks. And even if they did somehow trace me back to the hostel, how would they know we were here?"

"I don't know, but I recognize one of them," said Ada. "He was with Ms. North, Shukhov, and the others at my dad's prison."

"Maybe he's here to help us, like Shukhov?" Jace asked hopefully.

Ada shook her head. "He didn't say much, but his boss, Ms. Wang, did not seem to like me at all."

"Well, let's not draw attention to ourselves," said Cody.

Thankfully, the line for a taxi was short, so it was only a few minutes before they were on their way to the train station. They didn't see any more agents during the ride, Chinese or otherwise, and quickly boarded the train to Galway once they reached the station.

Jace leaned back into his seat and smiled with relief as the train pulled out. "Looks like we gave them the slip."

"It's too early to say that for sure," said Ada. "Until we know how they located us, we don't know when they'll do it again."

"Oh, yeah, I guess that's true." Jace looked a lot less relieved.

"It's possible they weren't even looking for us," said Cody.

"How so?" Ada asked.

"Maybe they figured out where the sub went, too. After all, we were using *their* data to find it."

"But if they already knew where it was, why wouldn't they go there right way?" asked Ada.

"What if they didn't know what to look for until Jace accidentally drew their attention to it?" asked Cody.

"No, you guys," Jace protested. "I swear I was like a ninja up in there."

"Keep telling yourself that," said Cody. "Meanwhile, I'm going to the loo."

After Cody had left to use the bathroom, Ada patted Jace's hand.

"It's okay, Jace. Nobody's perfect."

"Hm," said Jace.

He didn't look convinced, but Ada couldn't think of any other way the Chinese could have been tipped off. Regardless, they'd have to be extra watchful from now on.

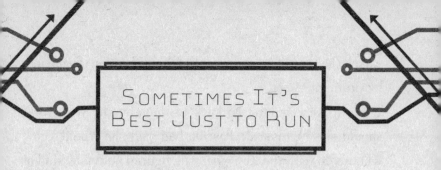

Coming from the almost-desolate Icelandic landscape, the Irish countryside was an explosion of green. The train sped past rolling hills and lush trees. There were small towns—villages, really—that had only a few roads, and neat little farms with herds of fluffy white sheep.

It was hard to believe that such a peaceful-looking land had been plagued by so much violence in the past. But Ada's father had told her about the Troubles, a bloody, thirty-year-long conflict that had divided Northern Ireland, which was part of the United Kingdom, and the Republic of Ireland, which was a separate country and a member of the European Union. The violence had ended long before Ada was born, but the two parts of Ireland were still separate, and perhaps they always would be.

"Some things are so terrible they can never be mended, chérie," her father had said sadly.

Ada wondered if her own life stood any chance of being mended. Maybe she could use the Key as leverage to get her father out of prison. Maybe that's why he'd sent her to get it. But no, he'd said he expected never to leave. And Remy Genet wasn't the type of person who said things he didn't mean just for dramatic effect.

So, if Ada couldn't go back to the way she was, what should she be instead? Pascale had said she would know what to do with the Key when she figured out what kind of person she wanted to be. But how could she decide something like that?

She looked to where Jace and Cody were sleeping in their seats across from her, and she felt a surge of warmth in her chest. She'd never really had any friends her own age before, and she found she really liked it. Whoever Ada became, she wanted to be the sort of person who could be friends with both of them. Maybe that was a start, at least.

Finally the train pulled into the covered station in Galway. Ada woke up Jace and Cody, and they walked out onto the platform. Her friends were still a little groggy, so Ada looked for the exit sign. She'd been to Galway before, and she thought she knew where the nearest youth hostel was. They could drop off their bags, then wander down Shop Street into the Latin Quarter, maybe grab dinner, then listen to some live music. Galway was known for its live music, and after all the running around they'd been doing, they deserved a relaxing night off before heading down to the Cliffs of Moher.

Then she saw the two Chinese agents walking down the platform in their black business suits and sunglasses.

"Okay, this way." She casually steered her sleepy friends in the opposite direction, so their backs were facing the agents.

"But the exit's the other way," protested Jace.

"Don't panic, but those same agents from Dublin are right behind us."

"*What?!*" Jace yelped.

"I said *don't* panic," hissed Ada. "And whatever you do, don't draw attention to us. I think there's another exit up ahead. Just keep walking and we'll get there."

They continued down the platform in silence. Ada could hear the sharp clap of the agents' dress shoes on the concrete behind them. They seemed to be falling in step, as if they were following but keeping their distance. Had Ada been spotted? She didn't dare turn around to check.

"Just keep walking," she muttered.

The footsteps behind them got slightly faster. Ada suspected the agents were trying to catch up to them without making it obvious.

"Though maybe walk a little faster . . ."

They picked up the pace, and so did the footsteps. Then a male voice with a Chinese accent called out:

"Ada Genet! Stop!"

"Run!" she barked.

The three broke into a sprint. A station attendant shouted, "Oi! No running on the platform!" but Ada could still hear the agents' footsteps behind them, so she kept running. They reached the exit and made it out into the station, where large clusters of people shuffled in all directions. Maybe they'd lose their pursuers in the crowds. She slowed down and tried to blend in, motioning for Cody and Jace to do the same.

But the people in the station were not, on the whole, particularly tall—and Jace was *very* tall. There also weren't many black people. The Chinese agents spotted them pretty quickly.

"Ms. Genet! Wait!" called the agent with slicked-back hair. His brow furrowed over his sunglasses, showing his increasing irritation.

"Go, go, go!" shouted Ada. They crashed through the throng of people, leaving a trail of disgruntled Irish locals expressing themselves with a great deal of salty language.

Ada and her friends ran out of the station and into the streets. Galway was a small costal city, with a curious mix of ancient medieval stone structures and modern buildings. It wasn't a highly populated city, not even as big as a midsized American one, like Baltimore. But there were always a lot of tourists in the downtown area, so the crowds were pretty thick. On one hand, that was a problem, because Ada had to constantly weave in and out of tour groups, which slowed her down.

On the other hand, it slowed down their pursuers as well.

Ada and her friends dashed across the lawns of Kennedy Park, interrupting a football game and leaping over several couples who were relaxing on blankets.

"Sorry! Sorry!" Jace kept saying as they went.

They raced across Eyre Square, dodging large sculptures and milling tourists, but the agents were still behind them. They needed to get out of the open and into the narrow, curvy streets where they could really give their followers the slip. Fortunately Ada knew just where to go. She turned down Williamsgate, then right on Abbeygate, with Jace and Cody close behind. They raced down the crowded sidewalk for a block, and then entered a pedestrian-only section. With no cars allowed, they could run right down the center of the narrow cobblestone street.

They reached Shop Street and turned left into an even narrower and more winding section. There weren't any cars, but there were even more people walking around. Most of the restaurants had tables and chairs outside, too. They had to weave through a space packed with tourists, some of whom were not entirely sober.

"Bloody kids!" shouted one old man.

At last the street curved south. For a moment, the agents

were out of view. Then, just past the curve, the street forked. Ada skidded to a halt, gasping as she tried to catch her breath. Then she grinned.

An eight-piece band was playing where the street split in two—a couple of guitars, a set of bongos, a cajon box drum, an accordion, a saxophone, a banjo, and a mandolin. They sounded great, but even better, they'd make excellent cover.

Ada grabbed Jace and dove behind the two percussionists, and Cody followed swiftly behind. They lay huddled on the grimy sidewalk, their chests heaving. Thankfully, the drummers just kept playing.

Ada caught a glimpse of the Chinese agents as they ran past and down one of the streets.

Once the song finished, the drummers turned around.

"You all right, lass?" the musician playing the box drum asked.

"We are now, thanks to you." She took a few euros out of her pocket and tossed them into the band's donation basket. "Merci beaucoup."

The man grinned. "Glad to be of service."

"That was way too close," said Cody as she climbed to her feet.

"I think I'm just going to lie here a while if that's all right with y'all," huffed Jace.

"Nope." Ada hauled him up. "They'll double back soon

enough. We need to find someplace to lie low for a while. Probably until tomorrow."

She looked sadly at the musicians, who were starting up another jaunty Irish tune. A relaxing evening of food and music out on the streets? Maybe next time. Whenever that would be . . .

Ada found a couple of nice Australian tourists who told them where the nearest youth hostel was.

"Are you sure we shouldn't just go straight to the cliffs now?" Cody glanced nervously around as they walked down the narrow streets.

Ada shook her head. "It would be dark by the time we got there, which would make it a lot harder to find clues. And it didn't look like there was anywhere cheap to stay even remotely within walking distance. We have to be smart about this. We'll be safe enough once we get to the hostel."

It wasn't like adults weren't allowed in youth hostels, but it was rare to see one. If the serious grown-up agents in their business suits did show up, they would draw immediate suspicion from just about everyone. What's more, people tended to look out for each other at youth hostels. There was a mellow sense of camaraderie, a shared spirit of adventure. In fact, a youth hostel might be the safest place in Galway for some underage runaways.

It was also, unfortunately, a pretty dull place to spend an evening. There were board games in the common area and a

TV with local channels, but that was about it. Ada and her friends ended up going to bed early out of sheer boredom.

The next morning, they went to a nearby restaurant for breakfast. Here Jace was finally able to experience the Full Irish: bacon, ham, sausage, fried egg, toast, baked beans, and . . .

"Okay, what *is* this?" Jace didn't wait for an answer before he bit into a round black disk that looked a little like a slice of dry sausage. "It's so good."

"It's blood pudding," said Ada.

Jace froze mid-chew. "I'm sorry?"

Cody grinned. "You heard her."

"But that's just, like, a nickname for it, right?" Jace clearly wanted that to be the case.

"It's mostly oatmeal soaked in cow blood, so no."

Jace winced. "You had to make it worse. Couldn't you at least say *beef* blood?"

"What's the difference?" asked Ada.

"Beef is something you eat. Cows are animals with big, sad brown eyes."

"He has carnivore guilt," said Cody.

"Ah." Ada never really understood the American relationship to meat. It seemed very complicated. As far as she was concerned, you ate it or you didn't. She didn't see much sense in eating it while pretending it was something else.

"Sorry for ruining your blood pudding," she said. "Should I also avoid mentioning that your delicious bacon is made from cute little piggies?"

Jace glared at her. "Yes, please."

Yet he somehow found the strength to finish his breakfast, including the blood pudding.

"Can we stop at a computer hardware shop?" he asked as he was mopping up the last globs of grease with a piece of toast. "The next time I hack into something, I want it to be impossible for someone to run a backtrace."

"Good idea," said Ada. "Let's think about what other supplies we should pick up before we head to the cliffs."

"Scuba gear, maybe?" asked Jace.

"Why scuba gear?" asked Cody.

"Well, I was thinking about how the trail for that sub just dead-ends into the cliffs. Maybe because it went into the cliffs."

"Like a cave?" asked Ada.

"Sure. I looked the cliffs up online and they're massive. Like seven hundred feet tall. So, what if there's a tunnel below the waterline? A sub could slip in there and surface in a cave. There could be like a whole supervillain lair down there."

"That's a great idea, Jace," said Ada.

"Yeah, so I was thinking we could hire a boat like last time and then, you know, scuba in through the tunnel."

Cody's eyes narrowed. "Have you ever gone scuba diving?"

"Um, no," said Jace.

"It's not something you can just do right away," she told him. "It takes a lot of practice to get the hang of it. You don't want your first time to be swimming through underwater tunnels in rough waters."

"Oh." Jace looked disappointed.

"Besides, we wouldn't be able to hire a boat to take us there," said Ada.

"Why not?" He looked even more let down.

"Too dangerous to get that close to the cliffs. It's shallow, the current is really strong, and one big wake could smash the boat right up against the rocks."

"Oh . . ."

"Which is why we'll need some climbing gear. Then I can just rappel down the side."

"Of *course* that's what you want to do," said Cody.

"You have a better idea?"

Cody shook her head.

"Samus . . ." Jace looked pained. "You did hear me when I said those cliffs are *seven hundred* feet tall, right?

Ada grinned. "I know! I can't wait!"

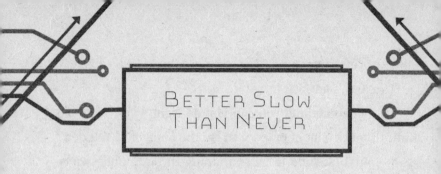

The Cliffs of Moher were a stretch of coastline over five miles long. They rose up from the Atlantic Ocean, from 390 feet at their shortest height to just over seven hundred feet at their tallest. That highest point, of course, was the section where the submarine had vanished from satellite.

Ada and her friends took a tour bus from Galway to the cliffs. Thankfully, there was no sign of their pursuers from yesterday.

Neither Jace nor Cody were willing to rappel a seven-hundred-foot sheer cliff, so Ada would be doing this particular job alone. At least Cody knew how to belay, which would make the whole thing a little safer.

The tour bus stopped in a massive parking lot. They walked along the path to the cliffs with the other tourists from the bus but got some strange looks. That was probably because Ada was wearing a full wetsuit and hauling a scuba tank and gear, while Jace carried a large duffel bag full of climbing equipment. That left Cody to carry all three of their regular bags.

The stretch of land between the parking lot and the cliff

edge was a wide, flat green interrupted only by a lonely stone tower in the distance. There was no fence or guardrail, just an open space that zoomed down seven hundred feet into crashing, frothing seawater.

"Oh man . . ." Jace's voice was almost a whimper as he looked over the edge.

"This is going to be awesome!" said Ada.

They put their gear down near the edge and got to work. First, they had to bury the anchor bolts into the rock, then set the top-rope anchor. Ada climbed into her harness. Then she fed the line through the rappelling device and set up an auto-block, so that if something went wrong with the device, she wouldn't go plummeting to certain death. Cody took her through a series of checks to make sure everything was in place. Then Ada pulled on her scuba tank and mask, and secured the small bag with her fins and waterproof flashlight to her waist.

"You ready?" asked Cody.

"She looks ready," said Jace.

Ada stepped over to the edge and peered down. Though her stomach squirmed at the sheer drop, Ada smiled. She used to hate that feeling as a little girl, but somewhere along the way she'd learned to love it.

"I'm ready," she told her friends.

"Be careful," said Jace.

"Buena suerte," said Cody, grabbing the slack end of the rope.

"On rappel," said Ada.

"Rappel on," replied Cody.

Ada crouched down at the edge, still facing her friends. Then she leaned back and started walking down the side of the cliff.

That first moment when there was nothing directly beneath her was always the scariest, and the squirm in her stomach became a lurch when the seven hundred feet of emptiness came into full view.

But years of training and experience quickly took over. Ada held on to the rope both above and below the rappel device and let herself hang there for a few moments until her heart no longer felt like it was going to bang out of her chest. In times like that, the line between excitement and terror was fuzzy. She was pretty sure she was feeling both. Although rappelling required less muscle than climbing, it was statistically more dangerous because there were a lot of things that could go wrong. So she waited until she felt calm again before beginning her descent.

In movies, people took big leaps down the sides of cliffs and buildings on their ropes, but in reality doing that was stupid and pointless. Sure, it looked cool, but it put a lot of strain on the equipment, which she'd need for the climb back up. Plus, there was an increased chance of losing control of the rope, and that was about the worst thing that could happen. As her father said, when it came to climbing, it was better to get there slowly than swiftly and painfully.

So Ada kept her hips parallel to the cliff face, her legs extended, and patiently fed the rope through the rappelling device.

As she got closer to the bottom, the sound of the water smashing against the rocks grew louder. She'd have to be careful she didn't get smashed herself once she got down there.

At last she reached a small outcropping that jutted above the surface of the water. Ada pounded a small spike into the cliff face, then took off all her climbing gear and hung it on the peg. She'd retrieve it for the climb back up.

Next she prepared her scuba gear, pulled on her fins, and took out her flashlight. She stared down into the frothy, dark water.

It was going to be *really* cold.

Ada took a deep breath to ready herself, then slid carefully into the water. It was even colder than she'd imagined. Her insides felt like they were contracting into a small, hard ball in her gut. At first it was even difficult to breathe. She waited until she got control of her lungs before she put on her mouthpiece and opened up the oxygen. One of the most important parts of scuba diving was controlled, regular breathing. Then she sank beneath the surface.

She pressed up against the cliff face, hoping the water couldn't bang her against it too badly if she was already there. She just had to be careful she didn't damage her scuba tank. Compressed oxygen had a tendency to explode on impact.

It was difficult to see in the murky water, even with the flashlight. The current pressed in on her, so she kept one hand on the cliff face to cushion herself as she swam forward and down.

Then, without warning, there was no cliff face. Her hand reached out and touched empty space. She hung there for a moment, groping blindly as the current swept out.

Then the water came rushing back, and she was whisked away into a dark underwater tunnel beneath the cliffs.

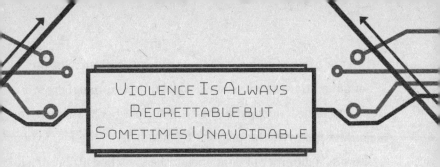

A da spun around in the darkness, the feeble beam from her flashlight showing nothing but swirling water and occasional glimpses of the rocky surface of the tunnel. By the time the current slowed down, she felt so disoriented that she didn't even know which way was up. Everywhere she looked was just water and rock. Her heart pounded so hard it hurt, and the mouthpiece of her regulator wasn't keeping up with her gasps of breath, so it felt like she was suffocating. The darkness pressed in all around her and icy panic coiled up her spine like a snake.

She closed her eyes. Did Samus Aran ever panic? No, she did not. Samus Aran focused on her job, and she got it done. Ada pictured the intergalactic bounty hunter in her mind, imagined her blue eyes staring with cool nonchalance through her helmet's visor at the hideous Space Pirates that surrounded her. Ada stared through her own scuba mask at the cold, dark water that swirled around her, and set her expression in that same look. It was a trick her father had taught her long ago. A way to face her fear even when she felt alone. Become what you want to be, and the feelings will follow.

After a few minutes, Ada was ready to continue. She might not quite know which way was up, but in a tunnel there were only two directions, and the current told her which way to go. She followed the passage for about ten minutes. When she saw a glimmer of light ahead, she switched off her flashlight and approached more slowly.

The tunnel opened out into a large underground pool. Ada could see the thick wooden posts of a dock along one side. And beside that was a submarine.

She was still underwater, so she couldn't see the whole thing, but the bottom was bright red and a little under a hundred and fifty feet long. It looked pretty old-fashioned, too. Like something that had been made in the 1960s or '70s. She supposed that made sense. Thieves couldn't often get their hands on the latest military tech, but older, decommissioned models were easier to come by if you knew the right people. In fact, getting a working nuclear reactor would probably have been harder than getting the sub itself.

Ada had no way of knowing if there was anyone around, so she didn't surface until she was safely concealed beneath the dock. Then she was finally able to look around.

Jace had been right. It was a proper supervillain lair. A huge open hangar had been dug out of the rock. It looked like one of those open-plan office buildings. In addition to desks, there was also a kitchen and several tables, and even an area with couches and a television. The entire thing was lit with massive LED lights that had been hung from the cave ceiling.

Ada's pulse was racing again, but this time from excitement rather than fear. Could the Key be here?

Although if the Key *was* there, she wouldn't be able to just waltz in and take it. Five people, all dressed in black tactical gear, occupied the space. Two were at computers, two were sitting on a couch watching a football match, and one was cooking in the kitchen. Ada could try to sneak around them, but the Key was small enough that any one of them could be carrying it around in their pocket. No, for a truly thorough search, she would have to incapacitate them all. And she didn't relish the idea of taking all five of them on at once, so she would have to handle them one at a time, without alerting the others.

Ada took off her scuba gear and stowed it beneath the dock. Then she climbed up and carefully assessed her options. The two men at the computers were facing in opposite directions and both wore headphones. They were the easiest targets, so she crept to them first. She unplugged a few cables near the office area and coiled them up. Then she found a stack of microfiber cloths used to clean computer screens and stuffed those in her pockets as well.

Now better equipped, she crawled into the aisle between the two men. Neither faced her, but she couldn't make any sudden movements or they might catch her in their peripheral vision.

Ada slowly rose up behind one man. Then she applied a blood choke hold by wrapping one arm around his neck and the other behind his head. A blood choke didn't actually press on the person's windpipe. In fact, they could continue to breathe normally. But the hold put pressure on both of the carotid arteries in their neck, which cut off the flow of blood to their brain. An unprepared person normally lost consciousness in about four seconds.

With his focus entirely on the video stream of an e-sports tournament, the man was certainly unprepared. As soon as he slumped over, Ada immediately released the hold. Cutting off blood to the brain for any longer would risk serious brain damage. Unfortunately, she only had about thirty seconds now before he regained consciousness. But that was enough time for her to tie him to his chair with some cables and stuff microfiber cloths in his mouth to keep him from calling for help.

Enough commotion would alert the others, so Ada worked quickly, cinching his wrists with the cable and finishing it with a surgeon's knot. Before the first man was awake, she'd already turned and begun the process with the guy at the other computer. Two down, three to go.

Of course, the other three would be more of a challenge. She could try using the blood choke hold on one of the two people on the couch, but since they were side by side, the second one would definitely notice. And the man standing in the kitchen was too tall to reach his neck with both arms.

The two men tied to computer chairs were already starting to come around, making muffled groans as they strained against the cables. It wouldn't take long before they alerted the others. She'd have to take a more direct approach.

Ada stepped up behind the man washing dishes at the sink. She tapped him on the shoulder, and when he turned around, she slammed her open palm into his chin. His head snapped back, then he crumpled. This was a much less gentle way to knock someone out. The human brain floated around inside the skull. When the head snapped back, the brain slammed first against one side of the skull, then bounced off and slammed against the other. If the person was hit hard enough, the brain could even ricochet back and forth a few times. That caused brain trauma, rendering them temporarily unconscious, but also potentially giving them a serious brain injury. Ada only used the technique when she couldn't think of anything else.

She caught him under the armpits before he hit the ground and injured himself even more, but he was so heavy that all she could do was slow his descent. She was about to tie him up, but the computer guys started yelling loud enough through their gags that the two watching TV noticed what was happening, so Ada was forced to abandon the kitchen guy.

It was a man and a woman by the TV, both in their thirties and very fit. The man immediately lunged at Ada, while the woman went for one of the guns on the table beside the couch. That was some good luck. If they'd *both* attacked Ada or scrambled after the guns, she wasn't sure she'd have been able to handle them together. But split up, they lost their advantage.

Naturally, Ada went for the woman with the gun first. The man was blocking the way, but his fists were up and his stance was wide, so she dove between his legs. He automatically went to protect his groin, which gave her an extra moment to vault over the couch and tackle the woman by her ankles. They fell in a heap, wrestling for the weapon. Ada jammed her pointer and middle finger into a pressure point on the woman's arm and the gun fell out of her suddenly numb hand.

Ada kicked the gun and it went skittering across the floor and into the water. The woman instinctively tried to reach for it as it flew past, and Ada used the distraction to strike the woman's temple with her sharp elbow. She hit her so hard, the woman's head bounced off the ground, knocking her out completely.

Ada winced at the sound of flesh hitting floor. "Sorry . . ."

She knew the woman had been planning to shoot her, but she still felt bad. There wasn't time to check on her, though, because the remaining attacker had just grabbed the other gun on the table.

Ada scrambled behind the couch as he unloaded several rounds.

"Come out, little girl," he said in Italian. "I promise I won't hurt you."

She didn't believe him, of course. But in her most innocent voice, she said, "Okay!" Then she tossed one of the couch pillows over the side.

He had great reflexes and immediately fired at the movement. That gave her a moment to side vault around the other end of the couch and slam both feet into his chest, knocking the wind out of him. He fell to the ground, gasping for air.

Ada stepped on his gun hand with one foot. Then she slowly drew back her other foot and gave him a swift, punishing kick to the face. This time she didn't feel so bad.

She quickly tied up the last two attackers, then began her search for the Key, starting with the guards' pockets.

But as she was rifling through the woman's pockets, she suddenly felt cold steel press against the back of her neck.

"You forgot to check the submarine," said a male voice.

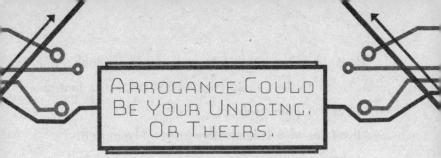

H ands up. Turn around."

Ada did as she was told. The man holding the gun looked only about eighteen, maybe twenty at the oldest. Barely a man, really. And he was smirking more like a bratty child than a hardened criminal.

"I suppose I should be impressed." He nodded to the unconscious guards. "You made it this far and took out all my men. Not bad for a spoiled little girl."

"*I'm* spoiled?" she asked.

"Of course. Daughter of the famous Remy Genet? You've had everything handed to you your whole life. If you weren't *at least* this good, I'd wonder if you were completely hopeless."

"So, it's not that I'm spoiled," sniped Ada. "It's that you're jealous."

He scowled. "Maybe I was once but not anymore. Now I have an even better mentor than that sentimental fool."

"Who?" asked Ada.

He went back to his smirk. Ada wondered if scowling and smirking was all he could do. "Wouldn't you like to know?"

He grabbed her by the arm and pulled her roughly to her feet. He might be young, but he was still over a foot taller than her and quite strong.

"I wonder what I should do with you," he mused.

"Let me go?" she suggested.

"You wish."

"Fight me fair and square?"

"Don't make me laugh."

"So you're afraid of getting your butt kicked by a little girl?"

The scowl came back. "Nice try, but you won't goad me into giving you an opening. In fact, I think I should just kill you. She said not to, but I can always make it look like one of the others did it. Of course, I'd have to kill them, too, so they couldn't deny it . . ."

He chewed on his lip as he considered. If he was really planning to kill her, why didn't he just get it over with? Not that she was complaining, but there had to be a reason, and that reason might just save her life. If his mentor didn't want her dead, that was the most likely angle to take.

"She? Is that your mentor?" asked Ada. "Maybe I've heard of her."

"I doubt it. She's too deep for goofballs like you and your dad."

"Try me."

He shrugged. "Professionally, she goes by the code name Mother Brain."

Ada's eyes widened. She'd never heard of a criminal who went by that name. At least, not one who existed in real life. "Mother Brain, as in the final boss in *Metroid*?"

"Obviously."

In the video game series, Mother Brain was the leader of a group of Space Pirates. Just like the name suggested, she was basically a giant brain, except with horns and an eyeball. She was also one of the most formidable villains in the series.

"So this Mother Brain is the one who stole the Hacker's Key?" asked Ada.

It couldn't be coincidence that this person had left a vintage copy of *Metroid* with her father's name on it at the scene of the crime. It was definitely someone he knew. And if this woman was a fan of the original game, then she was probably about the same age. That meant it might be someone he'd known for a long time. Maybe even since before Ada was born. She'd met a lot of her father's friends over the years, but no one who went by that name. Maybe she used to go by something else.

"Mother Brain stole the Key with *my* help," he snapped. "In fact, she couldn't have done it without me. So I don't know why she's so interested in you."

"She's interested in me?" asked Ada.

Her captor realized that he'd said too much and closed his mouth. But still, he hadn't killed her. What was holding him back? Did he see her as a rival, like Cody? That could be useful.

"What's your name?" she asked.

"I suppose it's only right that you know the name of the man who will kill you. I am Emile Neyrat."

"So, Emile, let me see if I have this right. You want to prove to this Mother Brain that you're better than me, even though you didn't have the advantages of my upbringing?"

"Exactly!" He looked pleased.

"And you plan to do this by making it seem like one of the men under your command got out of control and disobeyed her order not to kill me? How exactly is that going to make you look good?"

His eyes narrowed. "Well . . . it won't matter. You'll be dead, and I won't have to worry about competing with you anymore."

"Yeah, I guess there's no point in worrying about it when you've made it impossible to win."

"What are you talking about?"

"You'll never be able to prove that you're better than me if I'm dead. But I can understand why you'd want to do it that way. At least then you wouldn't risk actually losing to me, which would be so much worse."

"Please. I would never lose to a shrimp like you."

"Oh yeah?"

She was about to say something cool and provoking like *Prove it, sucker*, in hopes that despite what he'd said earlier, he *was* dumb enough to be goaded into giving her an opening.

But she didn't need to say anything. Because the guy in the kitchen that she hadn't had time to tie up was staggering to his feet. He was clearly concussed and grabbed the dish rack to steady himself. In his dazed state, he accidentally pulled the whole thing off the counter.

Plates and glasses smashed against the floor, and Emile glanced over at the noise. It was only a momentary distraction. But for someone like Ada, who had been drilling disarm moves since she was five, a moment was all she needed.

She used both hands to knock his weapon up and slightly to the left, while simultaneously ducking her head down and to the right. Then she grabbed his wrist with one hand while striking the gun barrel with the other. The gun went spinning and Emile cried out. She *may* have broken his trigger finger in the process.

But Ada wasn't about to let up just because of that. She followed up with an elbow to the jaw. He reeled back, leaving himself completely open, so she kicked him in the groin.

Emile fell to his knees with a wheeze and did not get back up. Ada grabbed one of the computer cables and tied his hands behind his back.

The kitchen guy was still stumbling around, so befuddled that she didn't even have to knock him out a second time when she tied him up.

She searched his pockets, then the other guards', but didn't find the Key. She searched everywhere else, even cutting open pillows, just in case. Still nothing.

"Where's the Key?" she asked Emile.

He just glared at her.

"Fine. Where's Mother Brain?"

"Like I'd tell you," he muttered.

"Or else you don't know," said Ada. "I bet she doesn't even trust you enough to tell you where she's going, does she?"

He didn't say anything more, so she gave up on him. He probably genuinely didn't know, anyway.

As she'd searched for the Key, Ada had kept nudging one of the computers to make sure it didn't go to sleep. Otherwise it would have probably logged out and then she wouldn't have been able to get access to it. Now, without anywhere else left to look, she sat down at the computer and began searching through the browser history. That's when she finally found a lead. Airline ticket searches for one-way flights from Dublin to Prague. Sure, it was pretty vague. But it was all she had right now. And the good news was, her father's sometimes-girlfriend, Reina, lived in Prague. Reina was amazing. She was like a cooler, funnier version of Ada's father. Once Ada and her friends got to Prague, they'd have all the help they needed to track down Mother Brain.

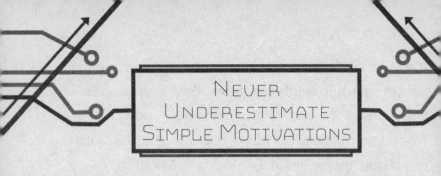

Ada wasn't sure what to do with Emile and the other guards. It was a secret base, so no one was just going to stumble across them, and she didn't want them to starve to death. After some thought, she decided to leave his hands tied behind his back but not secure him to anything. Eventually he'd inch his way over to one of his lackeys, and they'd be able to free each other. She *did* drag him as far from his people as she could and placed a bunch of heavy furniture between them because she didn't want him to get free too quickly and warn Mother Brain that Ada was homing in on her.

Once she was satisfied that Emile would eventually be able to escape, but with much difficulty, she retrieved her scuba gear and flashlight from where she'd stowed it under the dock, then headed back through the cave. Toward the end of the swim, when she was near the mouth and really fighting against the current, she pulled off the oxygen tank. She twisted around and pointed the tank behind her, then opened the valve. The oxygen tank sprayed out the last of its air in a big gush that sent her flying out of the cave.

She abandoned her scuba gear on the rocky ledge next to the ropes and climbing harness. She felt a little bad about that, but the ascent was going to be much more difficult, and she was already exhausted. The less weight she was carrying, the better.

She stepped into her harness and secured her ropes. Then she gave the line two hard tugs to signal to Cody that she was ready. Cody's job, as the belayer, was to hold the other end of the rope and pull in the slack as she climbed. And of course, in the unlikely event that Ada slipped, Cody would be there to stop her from falling to her death.

Typically the climber would call out, "On belay" when they were ready, and the belayer would respond, "Belay on" to let the climber know they could begin. Since there was no way Cody would hear her seven hundred feet up over the crashing of waves, they'd agreed ahead of time on two quick tugs of rope from Ada, followed by three tugs back from Cody. Ada waited a few nervous moments before she finally felt the rope lurch three times.

Now to make her ascent. Ada had been both looking forward to and dreading the climb. She hadn't mentioned this to her friends because she didn't want them to worry, but it would probably be the hardest one she'd ever done. Climbing was as much a strategic challenge as it was a physical effort. Buildings weren't that difficult, really. The surface was predictable. Windows, balconies, and archways all appeared at regular intervals. Once you figured out the pattern, you planned your route and executed it. Très facile. But natural surfaces were unpredictable. The first time you climbed one, every bit of progress was a surprise. You had to constantly adjust your plan, and sometimes if you encountered a particularly difficult bit of terrain, you had to climb back down a little ways and find a better route.

And that's how it was for Ada as she patiently climbed the Cliffs of Moher. The ocean winds pulled at her wet ponytail and chilled her to the bone. At the same time, the hot sun overhead caused her to sweat so badly it ran down her face and stung her eyes. Her arms and legs burned with fatigue and her whole body was starting to shake with exhaustion. Normally she would focus only on what was in front of her, but her weary mind began to drift to the hundreds of feet that now stretched below.

A little more than halfway up, Ada began to wonder if she could really do it. Could she really reach the top of the most challenging climb of her life, all on her own, after diving into a hidden cave and taking down a lair full of goons? She felt her resolve waver.

So she promised herself that once she got to Prague, she would make Reina take her to that place in Smíchov with the sweet dumplings. She recalled how tasty they were, and how much she was looking forward to seeing Reina again. That gave her the strength to continue.

At last Ada reached the ledge, then hauled herself up and collapsed in the soft grass.

"Wow, Samus, you actually did it," she heard Jace say.

"Yup." She lay there with her eyes closed for a little while, feeling the sun on her face as the wind dried her sweat. Then she looked up at Jace, who was holding the rope, and frowned. "Where's Cody?"

"Oh, she had to use the restroom," said Jace. "But she told me what to do if you signaled while she was gone."

"Huh." Ada couldn't decide if she would have preferred to know if she was climbing with an inexperienced belayer beforehand or not. Probably not.

"Honest, Samus, I had you," Jace said quickly.

She smiled. "I know, Jace."

"So?" he asked eagerly. "What did you find down there?"

"Just like you thought, a full-on supervillain hideout."

His eyes lit up. "Oh man, I wish I could have seen it. Tell me everything."

"You two can nerd out about evil lairs later," said Cody as she strolled toward them. "Did you find the Key?"

"No," said Ada. "But we're getting closer. The person who stole it goes by the alias Mother Brain."

"Like *Metroid*?" asked Jace.

"Exactly," said Ada.

"Hm," said Jace. "Ridley would have been a cooler choice."

"What are you nerds even talking about?" asked Cody.

"Doesn't matter," said Ada. "The point is, Mother Brain is supposedly some big mercenary who knows me and my dad. She's got secret bases, nuclear submarines, and who knows what else. She's extremely well-funded."

Cody frowned. "Clearly . . ."

"What?" Ada's eyes narrowed suspiciously. Was Cody getting tempted to switch sides?

"Nothing," Cody said quickly.

"It'd better be," Ada said ominously. "You might be able to speak fifteen languages, but I could think of at least fifteen ways to knock your teeth out if I thought you were double-crossing us."

"Whoa, now." Jace stepped between them. "Nobody needs to knock anybody's teeth out because nobody is double-crossing. *Isn't that right, Cody?*"

"Of course not," said Cody. "I just wish we had that kind of funding, all right? What's wrong with wanting to travel in a little more luxury?"

"It's indulgent," said Ada.

"Dios mío, you are so French!" Cody groaned. "And not even *fancy* French. You're like a mini Parisian snob who only wears

152

black and is *too cool* for expensive clothes and nice hotels. I bet that's exactly what your dad is like, and you're just a little blond copy of him. Why don't get your own personality, chiquita Remy?"

Ada stared at her. Where had this come from? Okay, sure, she may have threatened to knock Cody's teeth out, but that hadn't been personal. This was a personal attack.

And it stung more because there was some truth to it. Ada's father had a strong personality. She knew that. And maybe she idolized him a little too much. It was hard growing up with someone like him and no one else to balance things out. Hard to be anything other than what he was. She'd learned that when she went along with what he wanted, everything was happy and fun. If she questioned or challenged him, things weren't as fun. And there had been nowhere else to go, no one else to whom she might turn. People like Emile, who were jealous of her—they had no idea how hard it had been. And sometimes, how very lonely.

"So." Ada glared at Cody, her eyes like slivers of ice. "It's like that."

"Cody," said Jace, still standing between them. "You took that way too far."

Cody looked at Jace, then back at Ada, but she didn't apologize.

Jace gave Ada a pained smile. "Samus, I—"

"It's fine," Ada said quietly. "I'm glad I finally know what she really thinks of me."

"Well, I *already* knew what you think of me," snapped Cody.

"What do you mean?" asked Ada.

"I *mean* you've been judging me since the day we met. You think I'm shallow, frivolous, and scheming. You didn't even want me along."

"That *was* how I thought of you," admitted Ada. "But since we started traveling together, I changed my mind. In fact, I honestly thought we were becoming friends. I guess I was wrong about that."

Cody looked stunned. "Wait. You thought of me . . . as a friend?"

Ada was still hurt, and she didn't know if she wanted to give Cody the satisfaction of saying it again.

Jace once again interceded. "That's what she just said, Cody. So don't you feel like a jerk now?"

Cody closed her eyes for a moment and bit her lip. When she opened her eyes again, they were a little softer. "Okay. Maybe I *did* go too far. I . . . I'm sorry, Ada. I guess I'm not used to having actual friends. In this life, whatever you want to call it, there aren't a lot of chances to make friends, you know?"

Ada looked at her a moment, trying to decide if she believed this sudden change of heart. Finally she said, "Yeah. I haven't had a lot of friends, either."

There was a moment of silence. Then Jace cleared his throat.

"Soooo . . . are we good, ladies?"

Ada nodded. "We're good."

"Do we know where this Mother Brain person is, anyway?" asked Cody.

"Prague," said Ada. "And before you ask, we're taking the train."

Cody's eyes almost popped out of her head. "To *Prague*? That's like . . . *two days*!"

"Closer to one," said Ada. "But yeah, it's going to be a long trek."

"Is there a reason we're not flying?" asked Jace.

"Ada's worried that those Chinese agents found us in Dublin because they already somehow know our passport aliases and have us on some kind of watch list," said Cody.

"Exactly," said Ada. "Airports require names and IDs to be tracked for every flight, but trains don't. Once we get into Europe, they'll have no idea what our final destination is."

"It's going to take forever, though," Cody groaned.

"We'll get a sleeper car," said Ada.

At least Jace seemed pleased by that idea. "For real? Like in the movies? I've never been on one of those."

"Hooray," Cody said dryly. "The American is once again thrilled by the novelty of international travel."

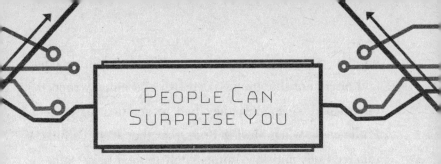

The journey to Prague began immediately. First, they took the bus back to Galway. Then it was another two and a half hours by train back to Dublin. From there, they boarded a ferry that was large enough to fit more than a hundred cars.

Ada always thought it was a strange sight, all those cars driving slowly in neat rows onto the wide, open cargo hold of the ship. Vehicles inside vehicles. Some people remained in their cars for the ferry ride, but the sensible ones climbed up into the passenger area where they could view the dark, choppy waters of the Irish Sea and breathe in its cold, salty air.

The ferry arrived in Holyhead, Wales, a little over three hours later. They had to show their passports when entering the United Kingdom, so if the Chinese government, or anyone else for that matter, had a trace on those names, they now knew that Ada and her friends were in the UK.

From Holyhead, they took a train through the English countryside to St. Pancras Station in London. Ada wished they could have stayed at least a day or two in London. She loved its odd mixture of ancient medieval and ultramodern, and of course the greasy fried fish and chips wrapped in newspaper cones. But they had to get to Prague before Emile could warn Mother Brain that they were coming, so Ada led Cody and Jace immediately to their next train.

St. Pancras Station was a massive, multilevel train station with curved glass ceilings and swarms of people. As they hurried to their connecting platform, Ada's eyes scanned the dense crowds that surrounded them. If the people pursuing them saw their names pop up in Holyhead, they would likely assume that they were heading to London. The train had taken about three and a half hours. Could their pursuers get agents to London in that amount of time? Ada didn't know . . .

"You look like someone who's worried about being spotted," Cody muttered to her as the three of them walked briskly through the station. "All that does is draw attention."

"You're right." Ada forced herself to slow down to a normal pace and keep her eyes forward. The station was so crowded that it would be difficult to pick them out from the masses. Unlike Galway station, there were plenty of tall people.

"I'm starving," said Jace.

"Right." Ada looked around for a classic fish-and-chips vendor, but all she saw were chain restaurants. Instead they grabbed the oddly flavored premade sandwiches that to Ada seemed unique to the UK, then boarded the train for Amsterdam.

"I promise once we get to Prague and meet up with Reina, we'll get some real food," Ada said. She collapsed into her seat and began peeling back the plastic on her triangular sandwich container.

"So what's this Reina like?" Jace asked. "I don't think you've ever mentioned her before."

"Reina's a cool Czech woman around my father's age. Sometimes they date."

"Sometimes?" Jace pulled off the cover of his tuna-and-sweetcorn sandwich, frowning down at it.

"Well, they're both intense people. Sometimes that means they get along really well. Sometimes it means they can't stand each other. I can never keep track of when they're dating, so I just call her my father's sometimes girlfriend."

"I guess that makes sense." Jace turned to Cody. "What about your parents?"

Cody froze in mid-chew. "Huh?" she said around her cheese-and-spring-onion sandwich.

"I just realized I don't really know anything about them," said Jace. "Are they alive? Are they together? You know my mom is dead and my dad is MIA. Ada's mom is MIA and her dad is locked up in supermax. So what about you?"

Cody's eyes darted around nervously. Ada didn't think she'd ever seen her so uncomfortable. "They're both alive."

"And?" asked Ada.

"And I know where they are."

"So are you going to go back to them when this is all over?" asked Jace.

Ada thought it was a reasonable enough question, but Cody stared at him like he'd just asked her if she planned on throwing herself into a tank full of hungry sharks.

"Um, no" was all she said.

"Do you not get along with your parents?" asked Ada.

"Why do you care?" snapped Cody.

"Because I thought we were working on being friends. I'm no expert, but I'm pretty sure friends are supposed to care about stuff like that."

"Samus, maybe we should lay off," said Jace, ever the peacemaker. "It's obvious she doesn't want to talk about personal stuff."

"Sure." Ada turned her attention to her egg, mayo, and cress sandwich without a lot of enthusiasm.

"My dad is a jerk," Cody said quietly without looking at them. "A really big jerk. And my mom refuses to leave him, so . . ." She shrugged. "So I left them both."

"You've been on your own for a while, I guess?" asked Jace.

"Yeah." She still didn't look at them. "A while."

Ada stared at Cody with new appreciation. No wonder it was so hard to get along with her. She was used to being on her own and probably didn't even know *how* to get along with other people. It was a strange idea, really. Cody could speak so many languages, and she was good at getting people to do things for her. She'd fooled those US soldiers and convinced the Icelandic captain to help them. Ada didn't understand how someone could communicate and manipulate people so well but couldn't get along with anyone as a regular person.

"Well, you're not alone anymore," Jace told Cody. "You've got us. Ain't that right, Samus?"

"Of course," said Ada.

Cody nodded. "Thanks."

They sat there eating their weird British sandwiches in silence for a little while.

Then Ada said, "You know, Cody, what little I remember about my mom, I think she's probably a jerk, too. So I get it."

Cody stared down at her sandwich. But a shy smile curled up at the corners of her mouth. "I don't think I ever expected to meet someone my own age who understood me as well as you do."

"Yeah." Ada felt the same. She wasn't sure she and Cody

would ever truly be friends. She still wasn't sure she even *liked* Cody all that much. But they'd both had such strange, lonely childhoods, and it was nice to have someone around who just . . . *got* it. Maybe Jace was right. Maybe *rivals* was exactly the right word for her relationship with Cody. And maybe that was a good thing.

The thing Ada liked best about trains was the rhythm. Unlike buses and cars, which often stopped or changed speed with traffic, trains moved at an even pace. She and her father had ridden trains often when she was little. She listened to the smooth, unvarying sound while staring out at the moonlit pastoral landscape and quickly fell asleep.

Sadly, she only got a few hours of rest before nature called. One of the minor but annoying challenges of traveling through so many time zones was that her body was always playing catch up.

It was still dark when she awoke somewhere between Berlin and Prague. These particular sleeper cars had small passenger compartments with two bunk beds on either side and a window and narrow aisle between. Ada was in one of the top bunks with Jace on the bunk beneath. Cody slept in the top bunk across from them. During the day, the beds could be folded up into seats, but performing double-duty meant that they weren't all that comfortable as either: The beds were too stiff and the seats too squishy. There were deluxe sleeper cars available with proper beds and private bathrooms with showers, but the money was starting to run low. Ada expected she'd be able to replenish their funds in Prague—either from Reina, or at her father's safe house. But it never hurt to be cautious, so she'd opted for the less expensive sleeper. Unfortunately, that meant she now had to trudge sleepily down the hallway to the public bathroom at the end of the car.

She was on her way back when she saw that the door to their cabin was not how she'd left it.

Snapping wide awake, Ada crept closer. She was certain she'd closed the door completely, but now it was open a crack. She tried to peek into the room, but all she could see was Jace sleeping in one of the lower bunks. She silently eased the door open and saw that there were two men hunched over their backpacks, which lay on the unoccupied lower bunk beneath Cody. The light from the hallway illuminated them enough that Ada could see it was the two Chinese agents who had chased them in Ireland. Unfortunately, the agents also noticed the additional light in the cabin. They both turned toward the door.

"Genet!" said the thin man with slicked-back hair.

Ada stepped back out into the hallway. She thought about rushing them, but she didn't like the odds against two well-trained, well-armed agents in a tiny room with minimal space for maneuvering. She also didn't know if Jace and

Cody would be a help, or merely hostages. Maybe she could—

"Genet!"

A different voice, this one American, drew her attention down the hallway.

A man and woman dressed in suits and looking very much like CIA agents were coming toward her. Were the Americans and Chinese working together? She really hoped not. Regardless, there was only one thing left to do now and one direction in which to do it. She ran down the car toward the rear of the train with four agents after her. At least she was drawing them away from her friends.

"Agent Zhao, what are you doing here?" demanded one of the Americans.

"I could ask you the same, Agent Watts!" said the thin Chinese agent with slicked-back hair.

"Let's just catch her, and then we'll work out the rest," said Watts.

"Agreed," said Zhao.

Ada had hoped they might start fighting each other, but apparently these agents were too professional for that. For now they were working together—to nab *her*. She ran faster.

The next car was a quiet car with traditional seats. Some passengers snoozed in their chairs and others worked in the dim lighting, their laptops bathing their faces in ghostly illumination. Ada thought about ducking into one of the empty seats and hoping the agents passed her by, but they were still too close. She'd need to be out of their view for that to work. She had to get more distance between them.

She jumped up and yanked down some of the suitcases stored in overhead bins so that they piled up in the aisle.

"Oi!"

"Zum Teufel!"

"Co to sakra!"

The passengers were understandably irritated.

"Pardon, pardon," she muttered as she ran.

She glanced back and saw that the agents were stumbling over the luggage and dealing with the irate people. It might give her enough time to hide in the next car.

But when she threw open the door, Ada immediately realized that wouldn't work. She'd arrived at the dining car. And at that time of night, it was nearly empty. There was no group she could blend in with. She ran on.

But as Ada passed the bar, she saw a bucket of ice near the edge. She knocked it down so that ice spilled all over the aisle.

"Dávej pozor!" yelled the bartender in Czech.

"Promiňte," Ada apologized. She wasn't fluent, but she knew the important words and phrases, like *hello*, *thank you*, *where is the bathroom?* and *sorry*. Ada didn't like causing trouble for employees any more than she liked disturbing innocent bystanders, but she hoped that at least some of the agents would slip on the ice cubes. A new idea was forming, but she'd need as much distance as possible to pull it off.

Though she didn't dare take the time to look back, Ada heard the agents burst into the dining car behind her. One of them let out a yelp as he slipped and fell. There was a cacophony of bumps and shouts as the agents behind either tripped over the fallen one or also slipped on the ice cubes themselves.

Ada yanked open the door between cars, slammed it shut behind her, and pulled open the one in front that led to the next car. Except instead of entering that car, she stepped to the side and clambered up the ladder to the roof of the dining car.

She lay flat on the roof and watched the junction until she saw all four agents cross over to the next car. She didn't want to risk them spotting her, so rather than hop down immediately, she decided to play it safe and get back to the sleeper car by rooftop.

Except in this case, safe still meant incredibly dangerous.

They weren't on a high-speed train. That would have made it impossible. Even so, this train was traveling at roughly a hundred miles per hour. Ada stomped one slow foot at a time, keeping her stance wide and her center of gravity low as she pushed against winds strong enough to register as a category two hurricane. The skin of her face felt like it was getting stretched back like a cartoon, and her eyes were tearing up so badly she could barely see. And it was really, *really* cold. The movies made it look fairly easy. Add one more to the list of things they got wrong.

She considered going inside through the quiet car but remembered all the people she had upset by knocking their luggage down and decided that another car length of freezing, fierce winds was still better than dealing with that.

Finally she reached the end of the quiet car and grasped the roof with both hands. Ada flipped down onto the junction, then hurried into the sleeper car. She didn't know if Jace and Cody were still asleep, or if they'd been woken up by the shouting. She just hoped they'd had the sense to stay put once Ada had drawn the agents away.

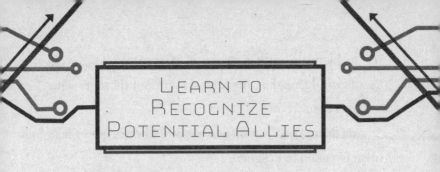

J ace stood in the aisle of the cabin looking anxious.

"Samus! There you are!"

Cody didn't look worried at all. She sat on the lower bunk and carefully brushed out her long chestnut hair.

"He wanted to go after you."

"Of course!" said Jace. "There were, like, four dudes chasing you."

Ada smiled. "Thanks, Jace, but it would have been really hard to keep dodging those guys *and* search the train for you. Plus, you might have gotten caught yourself."

"That's exactly what I told him," said Cody. "So what's the situation?"

"I'm not sure. Both Chinese and American agents are on this train. I have no idea how they figured out where we were, but we better get moving."

"We're stuck on a train with them," said Jace. "Where could we possibly go?"

"I led them in the opposite direction, which will buy us a little time," said Ada. "But, yeah, eventually they'll get to the end of the train and realize I doubled back. Our best bet is to try to blend in with a group of passengers and avoid the agents until Dresden, then get off without them noticing."

"And then what?"

Ada shrugged. "We'll figure it out. There's got to be a bus from Dresden to Prague."

"Ugh, buses are even worse than trains," said Cody.

Ada glared at her. "Or, you could keep the agents occupied while Jace and I take a bus. I'm sure they'd give you a *very* comfortable seat on the next flight back to Springfield."

"I'm *never* going back to that place," declared Cody.

"Well, then, unless you have a better idea, we take the bus," said Ada.

Cody heaved a tragic sigh. "Fine. Let's go mingle with the masses until we get to Dresden. Come on, there has to be *someone* worth sitting next to on this choo-choo train."

Ada understood that if they were going to gain the trust of a group of passengers to shelter them, even temporarily, Cody was their best bet. So she occupied herself with keeping an eye out for the agents as she and Jace followed Cody toward the front of the train and into the adjoining car.

Apparently none of the people in that car seemed "worth sitting next to" for Cody, because they moved on to the next, and the one after that. Finally they reached a first-class car where the seats weren't open, but enclosed in private cabins that fit six people each.

Cody grinned. "Now we're getting somewhere."

Ada sighed. "Of *course* you were looking for the first-class cabins."

"Trust me on this," said Cody.

The cabins were all to the left, with an aisle along the right side of the car. Each cabin had a door, but there was a window that allowed them to peek inside. Ada was surprised to see that a lot were empty.

"I guess I'm not the only one who thought first class was too expensive," she said.

"Couldn't we just hide in one of these?" asked Jace. "It looks like there's a curtain we could pull across the window."

"Too obvious," said Cody. "They see a private cabin with a closed curtain, that's the first thing they're going to check. We need . . ." Her eyes fell on one cabin window and she smiled again. "A deterrent!"

Ada and Jace followed her gaze and saw three girls lounging in one of the cabins. They looked to be in their late teens or early twenties and were speaking loudly in German. They had a lot of piercings and tattoos, and their clothes seemed to be mostly spikes, leather, and shredded denim.

"Them?" Jace asked skeptically. "I got to say, they don't look too friendly."

"Trust me, they're the ones," said Cody. "Just follow my lead."

She knocked on the door but then opened it before they had a chance to respond. She immediately began speaking to them rapidly in German. Their wary expressions shifted quickly to anger, and Ada was certain that Cody had just put them in an even worse spot than before.

But then one of them said, "*Ja, ja,*" and motioned for them to come into the cabin.

"What did you tell them?" Ada muttered to Cody.

"The truth," said Cody. "That some creepy guys were following us around."

Ada nodded. "Yeah, I guess that's what it comes down to."

The three girls moved toward the far window to give them some room. Ada sat down next to a girl with blond dreadlocks and black spacers in her ears. The luggage racks above were packed with guitars and drums. Ada wondered if these girls were in a punk band or something.

"Uh, hi, ladies," Jace said awkwardly.

"I am Hannah," said a dark-skinned girl in a heavy German accent. Her voice was chipper, which seemed at odds with the skull and demon tattoos on her bare arms.

"I am Greta," the blond beside Ada said, also in a heavy German accent. She pointed to a brown-haired girl with a rose tattoo on her face and a lip ring. "That is Nele. Her English is terrible, but she understands it okay."

"Hi!" Nele waved and gave them a sweet smile.

"So," said Hannah. "What is your names and where are you from?"

"I'm Cody, and I'm originally from Chile."

"Jace. I'm from America."

"Which America?" asked Greta.

Jace looked confused. "What do you mean, which one?"

"Sorry, this is our friend from the States," said Ada. "Sometimes they forget about all the other countries in North, South, and Central America."

Greta laughed. "Of course, of course. And you? Not from the US?"

Ada shrugged her shoulders. "I'm from all over."

"This is Ada, and she's so French it sometimes causes me pain," said Cody.

Ada glared at her.

"So who are these creepy guys following you?" asked Hannah.

There was another awkward pause as Ada, Cody, and Jace looked at each other. Should they lie? If so, what would they say?

Before they could answer, Ada heard familiar voices in the hallway.

Agent Zhao sounded irritated. "I could just as easily say that *you* lost her."

Ada crowded next to Jace in the corner where they

couldn't be seen through the door window. "They're here!" she whispered.

Cody slid into the other corner, then gave the three German girls a pleading look. "Just act like we're not here."

Hannah nodded, and the three began speaking loudly in German again. Ada worried they might be overdoing it a little, acting even more raucous than before, shoving each other and laughing. But she and Jace kept to their corner and out of sight. She pressed her ear against the wall so she could hear their pursuers better.

"Look, Zhao," came Agent Watts's voice. "She's got to be on this train *somewhere*, right? All I'm saying is that if, between the four of us, we can't find one little girl . . ."

There was a pause. Then, in a quieter voice, Zhao said, "Yes. It would not look good."

"Exactly," said Watts. "We're just doing a quick sweep now. If we don't find them, the Dresden stop is about ten minutes away. They'll probably try to make a run for it then and we grab them. If they decide to stay put instead, we'll have time before the next stop to do a thorough search cabin by cabin."

"Agreed," said Zhao.

Ada did not like what she was hearing. They'd be watching carefully at Dresden, so getting off would be difficult. But if they stayed on, they wouldn't be able to get away with just hiding in a cabin until they reached Prague. They needed a new plan.

"Did you check this cabin?" asked Zhao.

Ada didn't dare look, but it sounded like the agents were right on the other side of the door now.

Nele glanced through the window at the agents, and her sweet face twisted into something very scary. She shouted in German and made a rude gesture. Then all three girls broke into laughter.

"Teenagers . . ." Watts said sourly as the agents began to move on.

"Same the world over," agreed Zhao as their voices trailed away.

Ada sighed. "They're gone."

"That was them?" Hannah's eyes were alight with curiosity. "Those did not look like normal creepy guys. They looked like . . ."

"Like in the movies," said Greta, also clearly thrilled.

"CIA," agreed Nele.

As Ada gazed at their excited faces, she started to get an idea. It was a risk, but like her father said, sometimes you could just get a sense about people.

"They're government agents," she confirmed.

"Ada?" Cody didn't look like she agreed with this plan, but it was clearly too late.

"Which government?" asked Greta. "US?"

"US *and* China," said Ada.

The three German girls leaned in eagerly. Hannah asked, "Who *are* you kids? Are you fugitives or something?"

Jace winced. "I hadn't thought of it like that, but I guess so."

"We escaped from their military academy," said Ada. "They tried to control us, but we don't want to be tools of any government. So we escaped."

That was all true, of course, but Ada was framing it in a way she hoped would appeal to these girls. Judging by their reactions, she was right.

"That is so cool!" said Greta.

"What else can we do to help?" asked Hannah.

"Actually, there is one thing you might be able to do," said Ada. "Are you getting off in Dresden by any chance?"

A da, Jace, and Cody crowded around the window that looked out onto the Dresden platform. After a few moments, they saw Hannah, Greta, and Nele step off the train. Except Hannah was wearing Ada's coat, Greta was wearing Jace's, and Nele was wearing Cody's, all with hoods pulled up and hats on.

The four agents were on them in seconds. Agent Watts grabbed Hannah's arm and spun her around. When he got a look at her grinning face, his own went bright red and he began shouting at her. She shrugged and rolled her eyes, which only made him angrier.

Ada wished she could have watched his temper tantrum for longer, but the train was pulling away from the station, leaving the agents behind.

"Whew, that was close," said Jace.

"And you thought they looked scary," said Cody.

"I will never judge someone based on the number of holes in their face ever again," swore Jace.

"Well, are you happy?" Ada asked Cody.

"That I don't have to ride in a smelly old bus?" asked Cody. "Yes."

"How long until we get to Prague?" asked Jace.

"Maybe two hours," said Ada.

"You think we lost them for good now?" he asked.

Ada shook her head. "We still don't know how they found us in the first place, so we can't be sure they won't be able to do it again. We're missing something, but I don't know what."

"Yeah," said Jace. "It's almost like they have some kind of . . ."

He trailed off for a moment, and then his eyes went wide. "No! I'm so stupid!"

"What is it?" asked Cody.

"Ugh!" Jace looked frustrated in a way that Ada had never seen before. "I can't believe I didn't realize it before!"

"What, Jace?" asked Ada.

He clutched his head with both hands. "The day you escaped. I was called to the nurse's office. She said she'd been going over her medical records and realized that some students were behind on their tetanus shot."

"No . . ." said Ada.

Jace looked pained. "Yup."

"I don't get it," said Cody.

Jace turned to her. "It wasn't a tetanus shot. They must have implanted a subdermal tracker in my arm. I've been giving away our location this whole time."

"Ms. North knew I'd come back for you," said Ada.

"And she knew I'd *volunteer* to come along because it's the Hacker's Key." Jace's face was tense with anger and frustration. "She played me. How could I have not realized?"

"You didn't even know I'd escaped at that point," said Ada. "You can't blame yourself."

"It's just so obvious now."

"I know, I know," she said. "But like my father always says, there's no point in beating yourself up. The world will beat you up plenty on its own."

He laughed bitterly. "I guess that's right. Sorry, guys."

"The bigger question is how we stop them from tracking us, now that we know how they're doing it," said Ada.

"Easy." Cody rummaged around in her pack. "Subdermal. That means under the skin, right?" She pulled out a switchblade and flicked it open. "So we just cut it out."

"Whoa, whoa!" Jace held up his hands. "Why do you even have that?"

Cody shrugged as she looked down at the gleaming blade. "You never know when you're going to need a good knife." Then she looked back at Jace. "Like now, for instance."

"Nuh-uh." Jace shook his head, moving as far away as their cabin would allow. "There is no way you're cutting into me with an unsterilized knife."

"Don't be such a baby," said Cody. "It'll be fine."

"It will definitely *not* be fine."

"Jace, we have to stop them from following us," said Ada. "Can you think of another way to disable the tracker?"

He hesitated for a moment, but then relief shone in his face. "Yes! As a matter of fact, I can!"

"Before we get to Prague?" asked Ada. "We don't want them to know that's our destination."

"Two hours, you said?" He began to look through his own pack. "I can do that. Yeah. I can do it."

He sounded like he was trying to convince *himself*, as much as them, but Ada understood why he was reluctant to let Cody start carving into him. The way she handled her knife was a little too . . . eager.

Jace pulled out the electronic equipment he'd bought in Galway. It looked like he'd been building a new two-way radio transmitter, but he quickly dismantled most of it. For the next hour, Ada and Cody watched Jace work in tense silence. They didn't want to break his focus. Finally he sighed and held up a small circuit board with a couple wires hanging from it.

"Anybody got some gum?" he asked.

"Of course." Cody pulled a tin out of her pack and handed it to him.

Jace chewed up a piece as he rolled up his sleeve. Then he split the gum in two and used the pieces to stick the wires to either side of his bicep. He handed the attached circuit board to Ada. There was a small plastic button with a round watch battery underneath.

"Okay, when I say to, press down on that button, but only to the count of three. Then you let go."

Ada understood his plan. When she pressed the button, the battery would connect to the circuit board and an electric current would flow down one wire, through his arm, and into the wire on the other side, completing the circuit and sending a bolt of electricity through his arm. "You're going to fry the tracker?"

"I am."

"It's going to hurt," she said. "A lot."

"Better than getting carved up by Jason Voorhees over there." He nodded to Cody, who had been playing with her knife the whole time.

"Hey, now." Cody looked partly offended and partly pleased.

"And at least I won't have to worry about infection," he said.

"I guess not," said Ada. "Are you ready?"

Jace took a deep breath, then nodded.

Ada pressed the button, and Jace let out a loud yelp as his arm suddenly flailed around uncontrollably for three seconds. Then Ada released the button, and he slumped back into his seat, his arm limp at his side.

"That *really* hurt," he said.

"I told you." Ada gently peeled off the gummy wires. "Some minor electrical burns, but it doesn't seem too bad."

"I have something for burns, too." Cody handed Ada a tube of antibiotic ointment.

Ada carefully dabbed it onto the red welts on Jace's arm, then asked, "Can you move it?"

Jace lifted his arm gingerly. "It's really sore."

"Because of the intense muscle spasms," said Ada.

"How do we know it worked?" asked Cody.

"There's no way it could have survived that," said Jace. "And now they won't be able to follow us."

"Well, the Americans, anyway," said Ada.

"Excuse me?" Jace did not look pleased.

"Obviously that's how *they* found us, but what about the Chinese?"

"I thought the Americans and Chinese were working together," said Jace. "You said they were all in that room together talking about your father."

Ada shook her head. "It didn't sound like those agents, Watts and Zhao, expected to see each other."

"Oh great." Jace leaned back and closed his eyes.

"What do you think, Cody?" asked Ada.

"About what?"

"The Chinese," said Ada.

"What about them?" Her expression seemed confused.

"How they're tracking us, of course."

"Oh," Cody said. "No clue."

Ada looked at her a moment, and a new suspicion began to grow in her mind. Normally Cody was always trying to prove how savvy she was, but the moment Ada asked her about China, she went suddenly dense. Had she been tipping off the Chinese and blaming Jace's hacking? But if so, why?

Cody's eyes narrowed. "You're giving me a weird look. What are you thinking?"

It was only a guess, of course, but the more Ada thought about it, she realized it would explain a lot. Lengthy trips to the bathroom, especially while Ada was climbing down the cliffs. Cody could have found several opportunities to contact someone. But still, what was her motive? Maybe a payout from the Chinese once they got the Key?

Well, Cody might think she was fooling her, but two could play this game. Ada gave her rival a slow smile and shook her head. "Never mind. Just nerd stuff."

"Yeah, not interested." Cody turned away and became very focused on her nails.

"Hey, what about the Russians?" asked Jace.

"What about them?" asked Ada.

"We haven't seen them since Baltimore. But how did

that guy, Shukhov, even know to find us there right at that moment?

Ada frowned. She'd honestly forgotten about the Russians because they hadn't shown up since Baltimore. But it wasn't like them to let an opportunity like the Hacker's Key pass them by. Especially when both America and China were in the race. They would definitely turn up at some point, but when? And maybe more importantly, what would they do?

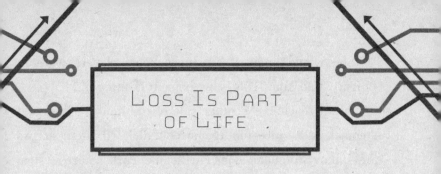

Prague was one of Ada's favorite cities in the world. It was cool without being pretentious, beautiful without being fussy, and despite a large tourism trade, quite cheap if you knew where go. The neighborhood of Old Town was filled with twisting cobblestone streets and Gothic cathedrals, but it was also the most tourist-heavy area. Once their train arrived, they didn't stay long. Instead, Ada led Jace and Cody to the underground metro and out to Smíchov, where Reina lived.

"I can't wait for you to meet her," Ada said as they left the metro and cut through the bright, bustling Nový Smíchov mall.

"And you're sure she's not going to be bothered that we're, you know, being chased by government agents from multiple countries?" asked Jace.

"No, of course not," said Ada. "Trust me. Reina can handle my father, so she can probably handle just about anything. She's a thief as well, although she mostly deals in art and artifacts."

"And you think she might know where this Mother Brain person is?" asked Cody.

"She would know if any major new players were in Prague," said Ada. "This is her home turf, after all."

They'd reached the other side of the mall by then and stepped back out onto the street. She led them across Štefánikov Street and along Portheimka Park, a narrow strip of green with a small dog run, then turned onto Preslova Street.

"We're nearly there," Ada said eagerly.

She was surprised at how excited she was. It had been two years since she'd seen Reina, so that was some of it. But even more than that, Reina possessed an unshakable calm. No matter what came at her, she never panicked or doubted herself. Ada was running from people who were tracking her in some way she didn't know, toward a criminal who was quite dangerous, if Emile was any indication. Reina's calm presence might be just what she needed.

When they reached the front door to Reina's apartment building, Ada pressed the buzzer. They waited for several minutes, but there was no answer.

"Maybe she's not home?" suggested Jace.

"I guess . . ." said Ada.

An elderly couple came out of the building. Ada smiled at them and said "Dobrý den," which was the polite and respectful way of saying hello in Czech. Once the old couple walked past her, Ada jammed her foot in the door before it closed.

"Come on." She held it open for her friends and motioned them inside.

The "inside" of the building wasn't actually indoors yet, however. It was a long tunnel that opened into a barren courtyard, where large trash receptacles lined one side. On the other was an iron door that was the actual entrance into the building.

"Now what?" asked Cody. "Are we going to wait for more people to come out?"

Ada shook her head. She went over to a corner of the courtyard and pried up one of the cobblestones. There were two keys underneath. One opened the iron gate, the other opened Reina's apartment. Ada grabbed them and hurried over to the entrance.

"Are you sure we should be letting ourselves in without permission?" asked Jace.

"She'll think it's hilarious," said Ada. "You'll see. We'll wait until she comes home, we'll have a good laugh, and then she'll take us out for sweet dumplings."

Once they were inside the building, Ada started climbing the spiral staircase, taking them two at a time.

"Isn't there an elevator?" puffed Jace.

Ada shrugged nonchalantly, like she'd seen Reina do so many times. "It's a Czech elevator."

"What does *that* mean?" asked Jace.

"It means," said Cody as she followed behind them, "that it either doesn't work, or it could break down at any moment, so it's best just to avoid it. Some former Communist countries pride themselves on being backward."

"Not backward," correct Ada. "*Austere.*"

Cody rolled her eyes. "Same thing."

Finally they reached Reina's apartment on the top floor. Ada unlocked the door and pushed it open.

"Hello? Reina?"

There was no answer, so Ada went inside, with Jace and Cody following close behind. The apartment hadn't changed much since the last time she'd been there. The central room had a small kitchen that Reina hardly ever used, and a smaller dinner table where they typically ate the takeout she bought instead of cooking. To the right was a living room with a television. To the left were the bathroom and bedroom. It wasn't fancy, because Reina wasn't flashy about her money, but it was neat and clean.

Except for the blood.

"Is that . . ." Jace started to say before trailing off.

There was a small red pool beside one of the chairs. A thin line of blood broke off from it, tracing a path to the closed bedroom door, as though something, or rather some-*one*, had been dragged across the floor.

"R-Reina?" Ada's voice quavered as she walked hesitantly

over to the bedroom door. She didn't want to open it, but she knew she had to. Even so, it took every ounce of will just to twist the knob. She pushed the door and it seemed to swing open in slow motion.

Reina lay on the bed, her unseeing eyes staring up at the ceiling. Her neck and chest were covered in dried blood. There was no doubt that she was dead and had been for a day at least.

"Reina . . ." Ada's voice cracked. She would have fallen over if Jace hadn't caught her.

"There's something stuffed in her mouth," Cody said quietly.

"I . . . I can't . . ." Ada struggled just to put words together. How could this have happened? Who could have done it? Her mind was swirling with questions, but they were sunk so deep in a fog of shock and sadness that she barely understood their meaning.

"I'll look." Cody seemed untroubled by the blood and dead body. Somewhere in the dark swirl of her horror, Ada wondered how often Cody had witnessed such things, if she could remain so calm about them.

Cody walked around the side of the bed to Reina's body and pulled a rolled piece of paper out of her mouth. She unfurled it and looked at it for a moment.

"It's a tourist brochure for Sedlec Ossuary," Cody said in a flat voice, as if she'd somehow shut down her emotions. "But there's something written on it in blood."

"W-wu." Ada tried to speak, but her throat was so dry. She swallowed and tried again. "What does it say?"

Cody looked at her with haunted eyes. "It says 'Mother is waiting.'"

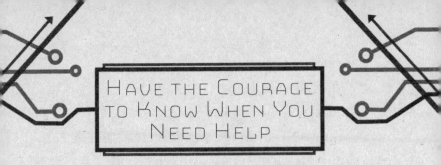

Ada and her friends sat in a cafe near Reina's apartment building and watched through the window as the local police arrived. Ada couldn't bear to think of her friend's body lying there unattended any longer, but she also knew she couldn't get tangled up in the investigation. So she'd made an anonymous call.

Now she looked down at the rumpled brochure for Sedlec Ossuary.

MOTHER IS WAITING . . .

The handwriting matched that of both the label on the Geiger counter package back in Baltimore and the *Metroid* game cartridge in Iceland. Mother Brain had left her a third, and possibly final, clue.

"She's calling you out," Cody said quietly, both hands cupped around a mug of herbal tea.

Ada nodded but said nothing.

"We're sure Mother Brain did this?" asked Jace.

"We're sure," said Cody.

"And the brochure means she's just waiting there for us?" Jace asked.

"For *me*," said Ada.

"Well, yeah, sure, but—"

"No, Jace. I'm the only one going."

Jace frowned. "Hold up. We're so close. There's no way I'm sitting this out. I'm going with you."

"Jace, you don't get it," said Ada. "Reina was good. *Really* good. Better than me. If Mother Brain got the drop on her, there's no way I'll be able to protect you."

"I'm not asking you to protect me."

Ada's expression hardened. She didn't want to do this to Jace. She knew it might hurt his feelings. But she didn't have a choice. "No? And if we get surrounded by a bunch of guys with machine guns, what will you do? Hack your way out of it? I'm sorry, Jace, but you'd just be a liability."

He looked like he wanted to protest, but he couldn't think of what to say. There wasn't anything he *could* say, really. It looked like that realization stung, but it was better he understand now.

"I'm totally cool with staying behind," said Cody. "There are criminals, and then there are psychos. I think it's pretty obvious which one this Mother Brain is."

Jace scowled. "Really? You're cool with letting Ada face this crazy person alone?"

"Of course not," said Cody. "Honestly, I think we should drop the whole thing. It's not worth it. A good thief knows when to cut and run. But Ada's not going to do that." She gave Ada a calm look. "Are you?"

"No," said Ada. This wasn't just about proving herself, making money, or saving the world from a techno-apocalypse anymore. Now it was personal.

"And I respect your choice," said Cody. "But I'm not dying for it."

"I understand," said Ada. "And I'm glad."

"For real?" Jace looked at her in disbelief.

"Pascale said that I needed to decide what kind of person I want to be," Ada said quietly. "That sounds really hard, but it's not."

She turned to Jace. "You are my best friend. In fact, you might be the only person I've ever truly been able to call my friend. You support me in a way I didn't know was even possible, and I count on you for so much."

She turned to Cody. "Honestly I don't know if we're friends, or if we ever could be. But that doesn't mean I don't care about you. You're still important to me. You make me question things in ways I hadn't before, and you challenge me to be better."

She looked back down at the bloody brochure in her hands. "I've never had people I care about like you two before. Now that I do, I know that I want to be the kind of person who protects the people they care about. I couldn't protect you if I took you to meet this murderer. At the same time, though, I want to be the kind of person who doesn't back down from doing the right thing just because they're scared. So to be the person I want to be, I have to face Mother Brain, and I have to go alone."

They sat there in silence for a moment.

Then Cody sighed. "Well, I guess this is goodbye, Frenchie."

"Seriously?" asked Jace. "Just like that?"

"What else am I going to do?" asked Cody. "No point in sticking around for Ada's suicide mission."

"I can't believe you—"

"It's okay," Ada interrupted him. "I get it."

Cody smiled. "I knew you would. Buena suerte, Ada. Maybe I'll see you again sometime."

Ada gave her a mischievous smile back. "I'm pretty sure we'll see each other again soon."

That unsettled Cody for a moment, but she quickly regained her composure. "Take it easy, Jace."

"Yeah, whatever." Jace didn't look at her.

Cody gazed at him for a moment, and Ada was pretty sure a little sadness slipped in through her carefully controlled expression. Then she nodded and left.

"Unbelievable." Jace's brow furrowed. "After everything we've been through, she splits just like that."

"She did what she promised to do, Jace," said Ada. "She

helped us find the Hacker's Key. Heck, she could have left after Iceland if she wanted, and she'd have still held up her end of the deal."

"I guess so . . ." His expression firmed. "Still, I'm not just leaving you. There's got to be *something* I can do to help."

"Oh, there definitely is. But you're not going to like it. *I* don't even like it, but this is too important for us to get fussy. I said I have to *go* alone, but that doesn't mean I have to *be* alone."

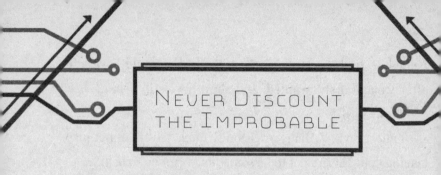

Ada rode the regional train to Kutná Hora, a small town that looked like it still had one foot in the Middle Ages. The train dropped her off at the edge of town, in a modern industrial area with wide roads paved in black asphalt. But as she walked, it was like going back in time. The straight roads narrowed to winding streets and the asphalt turned to ancient, weathered cobblestones. The buildings became old and worn, none rising higher than two or three stories. And off in the distance, at the top of a hill on the far side of town, was one of the largest cathedrals she had ever seen.

But Ada wasn't going to a fancy cathedral. She was going to Sedlec Ossuary, also known as the Bone Church. An appropriate place to meet a murderer.

The ossuary was located in the middle of a cemetery. It was still early afternoon, and the area was supposed to be a popular tourist attraction, but there was no one around. Mother Brain had apparently taken measures to make sure they weren't interrupted. Hopefully she hadn't just killed all the tourists in the area.

Ada followed the path through the cemetery, passing tombstones that were so old, the names on them had been worn away by the wind and rain. There was a small stone church in the center of the cemetery, and beside it a staircase that led belowground.

An ossuary was a container for the bones of the dead. But Sedlec Ossuary was unique. The skeletons of between forty thousand and seventy thousand people were housed in the large underground chamber, but they weren't buried. Nor were they merely in piles. These bones had been turned into art by a nineteenth-century carpenter named František Rint.

In each corner of the chamber there were bell-shaped structures made of bones that were well over six feet tall. The archways were lined with skulls strung up like garland, staring down at her with countless hollow eyes and empty grins. There was a giant chalice set against one wall, and a medieval coat of arms against another, both made ingeniously of various human bones.

In the center of the room hung a massive, eight-foot chandelier that was also made entirely from human bones. The chandelier was macabre, but it was also beautiful. Ada thought the way that Rint had used overlapping pelvic bones to form massive skeletal flowers was particularly inspired. Such an odd contrast would have delighted her father. She wondered if he had ever seen it. She hoped so. Because he would probably never get the chance now.

She sighed quietly. "Oh, Papa . . ."

"Your father proposed to me here."

The voice was strange, yet terrifyingly familiar. Ada turned toward the stone altar at the far end of the chamber to see a tall, slim woman in her forties with blond hair. She was dressed all in black. With her pale skin and hair and her cold blue eyes, she looked almost like a wraith.

Mother Brain was Lilith Genet.

"Mama . . ."

How could Ada not have realized? Her father had said, *Never underestimate family.* She'd thought maybe he'd meant himself, but no. He'd been warning her about her mother. He'd known, probably from the moment he saw the game cartridge, who had stolen the Hacker's Key.

Lilith smiled at Ada, although somehow it didn't reach her eyes. "Hello, Ada. My how you've grown."

"You killed Reina," said Ada.

"I've killed lots of people." Her mother didn't look bothered by it. "That's why your father and I split up, by the way. He just couldn't get past it."

"Because he's not a murderer."

"Because he's a weak, sentimental fool. While he was running around playing the gentleman thief, *I* was getting things done. Toppling old regimes, propping up new ones. Accomplishing real change all over the world. And of course making absurd amounts of money in the process. Now you have the chance to help me. To show me that you are more than your father's softheaded ideals."

"I—I don't understand."

Ada had always been afraid of her mother. Even as a little girl she'd understood that Lilith's cold indifference toward others was wrong. But those memories had been so old and faded, they'd seemed little more than a bad dream. The woman who now stood before her was even scarier than she remembered.

"I had to make sure you could handle yourself first, of course," said Lilith. "And my darling, you *flourished*. Recruiting a crew and utilizing their skill sets when expedient but going it alone when necessary . . ." She chuckled dryly. "Emile is quite upset with you, but I suspect he had it coming. He does have his uses, so I'm grateful you didn't kill him."

"So . . . this was all a test?" asked Ada. "To see if I was worthy to join your crew?"

"Yes, my darling Ada, and you've nearly passed."

Ada's eyes narrowed. "Nearly?"

Her mother held up a small black USB stick. It looked like a million others, but somehow Ada just knew it was the Hacker's Key.

"The world is full of weak, pathetic people who are so dependent on technology that they're helpless without it." Her mother's lips twisted into a snarl. "Once you help me deploy this, the weak will fall into chaos, and we, the strong, will sweep them aside."

"But people will die!" protested Ada.

Her mother shrugged. "I expect so. But really, anyone who can't survive without technology probably doesn't deserve to live."

"What about sick people in hospitals?" demanded Ada.

"Life is cruel. It's time for society to stop pretending it isn't. We'll never truly progress if we're always dragging around all that dead weight."

Ada stared in horror. How could her father have ever loved this woman? Lilith Genet was a monster.

"So how about it?" her mother asked. "Ready to join me in a brave new future?"

"Your recruitment pitch is terrible," Ada told her.

Her mother sighed. "I suppose I shouldn't be surprised. Remy has been filling your head with his nonsense for years. But don't worry. Once I've used the Key, you'll come around. You are my daughter, after all."

Ada squared her shoulders. "Except you won't be using the Key, because I'm going to take it from you."

Her mother laughed. "Right now?"

Ada nodded.

"Are you sure about that?"

She snapped her fingers and several men stepped out from behind the four bell-shaped piles of bones in the corners of the room.

"Now, now, my darling daughter. Surely you knew I wouldn't come alone."

"Neither did she," said a familiar voice with a Russian accent.

Ada turned to see Shukhov behind one of her mother's men, a gun pressed against the back of the man's head.

"Shukhov?" asked Ada. He had *not* been part of her plan. "How did you know where I was?"

Then Cody stepped out from behind him and waved. "Hey, Frenchie."

Ada's eyes widened. "Cody? I was pretty sure you were leaking our location, but I figured you were working with the Chinese."

"She was." Ms. Wang's voice came from one of the other corners. Agent Zhao stood next to her, holding a gun to the man positioned there. *This* was who Ada had expected to show up.

Ms. Wang gave Cody a cold look. "Ms. Francesco was gathering intel for us on the true nature of Springfield Military Reform School, but apparently when this whole debacle began, she received a better offer."

"How many times have you flipped?" Ada asked Cody, more impressed than offended. In fact, it actually made her feel better that she wasn't the only one Cody had turned on.

Cody shrugged and smiled sheepishly. "Don't hate the player, hate the game."

Ada sighed. Really, it was classic Cody.

She turned back to Ms. Wang. "So if Cody wasn't working for you anymore, how *did* you track us?"

Ms. Wang smiled briefly. "Ms. Francesco may be talented with languages, but she has much to learn about encryption. Once we realized she'd turned on us, it was not difficult to intercept her communications with Shukhov."

"And when did those start?" asked Ada.

"Iceland," admitted Cody. "After what he pulled in Baltimore Airport, I knew he was someone I wanted to work with." Her brow furrowed and she looked genuinely concerned. "No hard feelings, right, Ada? You understand. It's just business. I'm getting a *big* payout for this."

"Assuming Shukhov actually gets the Key," Ada pointed out.

Cody winced. "Yeah."

"That won't happen," Ms. Wang said firmly. "In fact, the Chinese government believes *no one* should have it. The Key poses too much of a risk and should be destroyed."

"Don't be a fool, Wang," said Shukhov. "At the rate AI development is progressing, we'll need it someday. Probably sooner than you think."

Ada's mother cleared her throat. "You're both arguing as if you already possess the Key, but you have only two of my men. We're still very much in a standoff."

"Actually, you're not." Ms. North stepped out from behind the third tower of bones and pressed her gun against the back of that man. A moment later, Agent Watts covered the fourth and final man.

"Special Agent North?" Shukhov did not look pleased to see her.

"Hello, Anton." As always, Ms. North only smiled when someone else was in trouble. "What was that about you taking the Key?"

He winced. "Just a bit of Russian humor, of course."

"Hmm," said Ms. North. "And what about you, Cody? Working for the Chinese *and* the Russians? When we get back to Springfield, you and I are going to have a very long talk."

"Actually, Agent North," said Shukhov, "Ms. Francesco has requested asylum in Russia. She will be coming with me."

"I see." Ms. North did not look happy about that at all.

"How did *you* find your way here, Agent North?" asked Ms. Wang. "I thought your tracker had been disabled."

"Oh, Ada invited me, of course."

"*What?*" Lilith Genet had kept her calm, even after Ms. North had shown up, but now she looked truly shocked. "That . . . can't be true. Ada, you didn't!"

"I did, Mama," said Ada. "What do you think Jace was doing this whole time?"

Jace peeked out from behind Ms. North and waved. Then his eyes got large. "Oh . . . kay, there are a lot of guns being pointed around . . ." Then he quickly ducked back behind her.

"You called the US government on me?" Ada's mother took a furious step toward her. "Even Remy would be outraged!"

"Maybe so," said Ada. "But I'm not my father any more than I am you. I'm my own person, and only I get to decide who that is. I realized that the best way to keep my friends safe and get the Key was to ask for help. So I did what I had to do."

"It took a lot of guts, Lilith," said Ms. North. "You should be proud of your daughter."

Lilith Genet sneered. "I am disgusted. And to think I actually hoped she would . . ." She shook her head, then shouted, "Lights!"

In what felt to Ada like slow motion, her mother tossed the Hacker's Key up into the air. Cody, Ms. Wang, Jace, and

Ada, the only people not holding one of the goons, converged on the Key.

Then the lights went out.

In the sudden darkness, they crashed into one another.

The lights came back on to reveal all four of them lying in a heap on the floor.

Lilith Genet was gone.

But Ada spotted the Key on the ground. She snatched it up and leapt to her feet.

"Got it!"

"Ah, Ms. Genet! Why don't you give that to me?" Shukhov offered her his warmest smile as he struggled to his feet.

"No, it's too dangerous!" Ms. Wang jumped up. "For the safety of the world, destroy it!"

Ada looked down at the small, unremarkable thumb flash drive. In that moment, there was so much power in her hand. She could do anything. Have anything. *Be* anything. But now she knew what she wanted to be. And it didn't require a weapon of mass destruction.

She turned to Ms. North.

"Our deal still good, even though my mother escaped?"

Ms. North nodded, her glasses glinting in the light of the bone chandelier. "It is."

Ada turned to Cody. "I guess you're not getting that big payout now. No hard feelings, right?"

Cody grinned. "None at all, Frenchie. That's how it goes sometimes."

Ada walked over to Ms. North and handed her the Key. "Make sure the UN actually has some decent security measures this time."

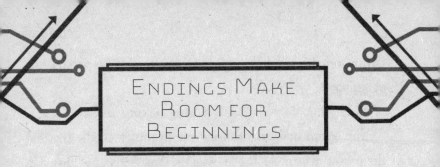

"Is it bread or is it dumplings?" asked Jace as he sat with Ada and Ms. North in a small restaurant in Prague. He stared down at his steaming plate of Cesky gulas, or Czech goulash. "I just don't know."

"It's houskové knedlíky," said Ms. North. "Which means 'bread dumplings.' So I suppose it's both."

"Whatever it is, it's good." He speared a thick slab of gravy-soaked beef with his fork.

"This was Reina's favorite restaurant," Ada said quietly as she stirred her own fork around in the gravy. She didn't feel like eating.

"I'm sorry about your friend," Ms. North said. "If it's any consolation, there wasn't anything you could have done to stop your mother."

Ada nodded. Ms. North was the last person she wanted to talk to about that.

Instead she asked, "So, what's going to happen to Cody?"

"I can't contest her asylum claim, so she's definitely going to Russia," said Ms. North. "I have no idea what Shukhov's plans are for her, but she's far too skilled for him to leave her sitting on the sidelines long. I expect we'll be seeing her again soon."

"And what about us?" asked Jace, looking uneasy.

Ms. North nodded. "You led me to the Hacker's Key and the person who stole it. That was the deal. I may not have gotten one, but at least I got the other. You won't get any demerits for escaping the school, and I'll wipe the demerits you currently have off your records."

"So it's back to Springfield, huh?"

Jace didn't look thrilled. Ada felt the same way. They'd gotten a taste of freedom and adventure, and now it was being taken away from them again. Even if they weren't in trouble, having to go back to the school seemed like punishment enough.

Ms. North swirled the coffee at the bottom of her cup and an unfamiliar smile appeared on her lips. It looked almost . . . nice.

"Actually, I wanted to talk to you two about that."

Ada and Jace perked up. Was there a possibility that they wouldn't have to go back?

"Now, you're both minors and wards of the federal government, so you must remain students of Springfield Military Reform School," she said. "However, that doesn't mean you must stay in Springfield."

"What do you mean?" Ada asked.

"You're both B Class."

"Barely," muttered Ada.

Ms. North nodded. "And you're obviously aware of the dreaded C Class."

"Of course," said Jace.

"Have either of you ever wondered where the A Class students are?"

Ada and Jace looked at each other, their eyes wide. Ada supposed she'd occasionally wondered why she never saw any of them but assumed they were just on a different floor.

Ms. North continued. "There are some young people with astonishing skills, who sadly have used those skills for illegal gains. Usually it's because of how they were raised. Many of them are in B Class at Springfield Military Reform School. But every now and then, one or two of those students prove that they've renounced their criminal upbringings. Say, for example, by stopping an international terrorist threat. For those students, we have a sort of . . . off-campus program, with a lot more . . . hands-on experience. A place where they can really grow and challenge themselves."

"You mean, like, a secret agent school?" asked Jace, his eyes wide.

Ms. North shrugged. "Something like that. So what do you think? Interested in joining the A Class?"

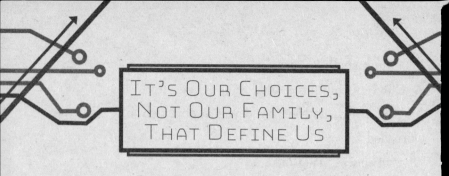

IT'S OUR CHOICES, NOT OUR FAMILY, THAT DEFINE US

D o you . . . trust Ms. North, chérie?" asked Ada's father, his expression carefully neutral.

Ada was back where her adventure had begun, sitting on the other side of a plexiglass wall from her father.

"Of course not, Papa," she said.

He nodded, looking pleased. "But you have accepted her offer?"

"Yes, Papa. Jace and I fly out tonight. I'm not supposed to tell you where. Sorry."

He vehemently shook his head. "There's nothing to be sorry about."

"Even though I'm going to be working for the US government?"

He shrugged. "For now. You learn what you can, then you decide what to do with your life from there. At least you won't be stuck in that *school*."

"Mama said even you would be angry that I was working with Ms. North."

"She was wrong, as she is about most things," said her father. "You made a difficult choice and swallowed your pride

210

for the sake of your team and your mission, as a leader should. I am very proud of you."

She smiled gratefully. "Thank you for understanding, Papa."

"As for Reina . . ." Ada's father pressed his hand against the plexiglass, his eyes moist. "I wish I could have . . ." He swallowed hard and shook his head. "I'm sorry you had to see her like that."

Ada's chest tightened, and she reached out to press her own palm against the glass, matching his. Maybe it was her imagination, but she thought she could feel his warmth, ever so slightly.

"I miss you, Papa," she said quietly.

He smiled through teary eyes. "That is understandable. I am pretty great, no?"

She gave a soft laugh. "You're okay, I guess."

"And obviously I'm not going anywhere. So you go, have your own adventures now, and I'll eagerly await the next time you come to tell me about them."

"I will, Papa."

She was not a thief like her father and definitely not a murderer like her mother. Perhaps she still didn't fully know what she was yet, but she planned to find out. On her own.

A NOTE FROM
THE AUTHOR

All the characters in this story are fictional, but nearly all the places, including the Cliffs of Moher and the Bone Church, are real. The only exceptions are the supermax prison holding Remy Genet and the Springfield Military Reform School. Likewise, nearly all the science and technology aspects of the story are also real, with the notable exception of the Hacker's Key itself. Sadly, when our AI overlords come for us, we'll need to find another solution.

ACKNOWLEDGMENTS

I love traveling and do it as often as I can. Nearly every location in this book is somewhere that I have been. I also like traveling with friends, and I am grateful for those brave souls willing to accompany me. Thank you to Darren Focareta for being my travel buddy in Iceland and Ireland, and Zach Morris for hanging out with me in Prague and Kutná Hora. And an *extra* big thank-you to Stana Benestova for not only letting me stay at her flat in Smíchov for free but graciously allowing me to set a fictional murder there. Thanks also to my sons, Zane and Logan Skovron, for keeping me up to date on all things *Dragon Ball* and *Super Smash Bros.* (Zelda is still my main; I don't care how low her rank is or how often I lose.).

I also want to thank my editor, Zachary Clark, who has been so enthusiastic and wise throughout this process, as well as David Levithan, who convinced me to write a middle-grade book in the first place. And of course I must thank my agent, Jill Grinberg, and the whole JGLM team, because they are always the bedrock of my support.

About the Author

Jon Skovron is the author of several young adult novels, including *Misfit* and *Man Made Boy*, as well as epic fantasy novels for adults such as *Hope and Red* and *The Ranger of Marzanna*. *The Hacker's Key* is his first middle-grade novel, but he had a lot of fun with it, so he'll probably write more.

Jon lives with his two sons and two cats just outside Washington, DC. You can find him online at jonskovron.com. You probably won't find him playing *Smash* online, however, because honestly he's more of a *Splatoon* guy.